# ÁTCO & Grass

## and other short stories

# Jim Jackson

Best Wishes to Andrew & Liz Jim

Typeset by Jonathan Downes,
Cover and Layout by SPiderKaT for CFZ Communications
Using Microsoft Word 2000, Microsoft Publisher 2000, Adobe Photoshop CS.

First published in Great Britain by CFZ Press

**CFZ Publishing Group**
**Myrtle Cottage**
**Woolsery**
**Bideford**
**North Devon**
**EX39 5QR**

© CFZ MMXIV

# ISBN: 978-1-909488-22-9

# CONTENTS

## ATCO & Grass and other short stories

# ATCO

I n a sane or saner world the two men might have been firm friends. They both attended the same village school, both were farmers and shared many of the same interests in life such as real ale and motorcycle motocross, which was called scrambling in those days.

Their mutual hatred was sparked by a fierce playground fight, its cause long forgotten which smouldered through puberty and burst into flames when they dated the same girls as young men. The breeze which fanned the fire into an inferno was the arrival in the village of a new girl. An elfin child of the valleys and the daughter of the new postmaster. She was a cracker. I even took her out once myself. Pretty as a picture, and as shallow as a bird bath in August. There was something else too, although I couldn't put my finger on it at the time. A feeling that there was more than a little streak of nastiness, cruelty or selfishness in her makeup.

Characteristics that were well hidden and easily overlooked by any young farmer whose attention was elsewhere, dwelling perhaps on suspender belts and higher things.

Having dipped her toe, metaphorically speaking, into the local gene pool, Caroline decided that the burly, quietly spoken introvert Oliver Banks, was the man for her. He had a good income from his small farm, a collection of off-road motorcycles and a Norton Dominator 99-SS. Now if that is not enough to turn a maiden's head, I don't know what is.

The other character in this story, and the unlucky suitor for Caroline's hand, was the big, bluff, and - some would say - vulgar extrovert, Billy Boyd. At school he was known as a bully boy, which gives you some idea of the stamp of the man. How it must have galled him to see his rival walking hand in hand or sitting quietly beside the fire in the *Farmers' Arms* with Caroline, gazing into each other's eyes over the two halves of cider. What was an ongoing feature of this relationship was the nauseating habit which they had acquired of pausing every so often when one would say "together" and the other would answer "always", and that's how it might have stayed; one farmer gagging on romantic honey the other choking on jealous bile. Except that is, for an unexpected marriage and a premature death in the adjacent village, the details of which will make a whole new story, but the outcome of this bereavement was that Billy Boyd inherited a large farm contiguous to his own and a substantial sum of ready money.

Having lashed out on those things which are close to a farmer's heart; a new tractor, a new shotgun and new boots, he also brought back from his first visit to London something designed to turn heads. An electric blue, heavily chromed and customised Harley Davidson. The very sound of it sang of testosterone, thump, thump thump, thump.

It was about that time that Emily Williamson, the postmaster's wife and Caroline's mother, took her daughter to one side, sat her down in the quiet of their best room and explained to her calmly and carefully the facts of life. Not about the birds and the bees. I daresay Caroline could have taught her mother a thing or two. No, she revealed to her daughter the inner secrets of life-sustaining Pounds and P's, which of course is far more interesting to a postmaster's wife of 23 years than the primeval antics of the birds and the bees. In her naivety and innocence, Caroline had no conception of yield per acre, cash flow or return on investment, and her mother soon put her right. Which was cruel I suppose, and set her tiny mind in a whirl. With half an eye she could picture herself holding the baby she might have had with Oliver, in her arms before a cosy kitchen fire. With the other half she saw herself in a long red silk dress stepping out of a Daimler to attend the Lord Lieutenants Ball with Billy. Quite naturally she dithered and prayed to God for a sign. It came soon enough with a tumper te tump te tump of Billy's Harley ticking over at the traffic lights outside the Post Office. From that moment on, the futures of three people were set in stone.

Oliver, his Norton all aglow and his hair bright with Brylcreem, called for Caroline just as a lazy sun laid itself to rest over the treetop fringe of the long hill known as Broken Spine. Even a man such as he, genetically programmed to be sensitive to the wants and needs of turnips and parsnips rather than people, could not fail to sense that something had intruded between them. He remained in ignorance not long. Just as he was about to utter the mystical invocation "together" and had every reason to expect the usual reply "always", she let him have it straight from the shoulder, both barrels. She might just as well have used a shotgun for the damage she inflicted. Not only was she no longer his girl. Bang! Right barrel, but she had transferred her affection overnight to Billy Boyd. Bang! Left barrel. Turning on his heel, he strode away and - quickly kick-starting his Norton, and with greater restraint that I would have shown - rode off into the twilight.

Strong introverts like Oliver don't shown their emotions much, just draw their heads into their shell to brood in silent contemplation of the vagaries of love and the unfairness of this cruel world. Upon his return home, he skinned and gutted two rabbits, polished off an open bottle of whisky and did irrevocable damage to a second, before falling asleep in his cradle of misery.

In contrast, Billy Boyd was full of himself and with reason. He had the prettiest girl in the village all to himself, a Harley Davidson which was the envy of all, and more money than a man of his class, education, aspirations and imagination knew what to do with.

It is true that money can't buy friendship, but Billy gave it a good try. It was bordering on the pathetic to see him stride into a pub to buy round after round of drinks for his sycophant circle of new friends who hung upon his every word, be it about motorcycles, girls or farming.

I was seated in the saloon bar at the *Farmer's Arms* with my solicitor Reg Beddis discussing the lease of a flat I was about to buy over in Midwych. Oliver Banks sat on his own in the far corner nursing a pint in one hand, and a dark rum in the other. "Poor bugger", says Reg. "Time he snapped out of it". Above the bar a black and white TV was showing motocross racing. As if stepping down from the screen Billy Boyd and a bunch of his cronies walked into the bar covered in oil and grime from a private meet of their own. The landlord, Mike Pearson, would have barred them except that Billy Boyd was spending money like water since his change of circumstances.

Mike, seeing these guys tearing round the circuit with clods of mud being thrown up by their wheels and splattering the TV camera lens, says for no particular reason, "I'll bet that they couldn't ride their bikes over a real piece of sticky ground like the patch off The Shield behind Hickeys Farm".

"I'll bet Sammy Miller on his BSA 500 could do it", says one of the bikers. "It's impossible", says another. "I'll tell you its just so much dirty water down there with the skin of mud and weeds on the surface why some people say that it's bottomless or at least 20 feet deep". "20 feet, my eye", said one of the new fellows with Triumph on his T-shirt.

"It can't be deeper there than 6 inches or so, any deeper and it would seep away through the fissure in the rock, which runs all the way down to Morton's pool. Why, there's a trickle of water runs down there all the year round, you know where I mean?"

"Now that really would be impossible. I mean, over The Shield, through the bog, down the fissure, through the pool round the rocky ground by Larkspur Stone, up over Kennel Rise, that's all clay that is, dead slippery in the winter, back through the pool from the south and across The Shield with its so-called bottomless bog".

"Cor Jesus, that is something I should like to see, but for one thing - it can't be done".

"Dave Bickers could do it, or Arthur Lampkin, Vic Eastwood or the Swede, Timo – something or the other".

"Well I'll bet you £100 even money that it can't be done by anybody", said Mike who rode a bit in his youth and knows his racing.

"I'll do even better than that," says Billy Boyd. "I'll bet you a thousand to one that it can't be done, not by your Swede, not by no-one."

Well, the hot blood of consensus in the room seemed to coagulate around Billy's respected opinion and the bar fell unnaturally quiet for a bit, until the silence was broken by an edgy voice which fell like a medieval mailed gauntlet at Billy's feet.

"I don't believe you mean that, it's just the drink talking, you always have been full of piss and wind Billy Boyd".

Whoo! Now here was something to see on a winter's afternoon, big Oliver Banks had found a voice and had decided to lock horns with Billy Boyd, no small man himself and unaccustomed to being contradicted or called a liar in public, in front of his friends. Things could have got rather hairy at that moment, but Billy - seeing Oliver rise unsteadily to his feet - said, "Well Ollie, you know I'm a man of my word, and I said a thousand to one and a thousand to one I meant. How much do you wanna bet"?

On stiff and unsteady legs, Oliver walked over to me and my solicitor friend, Reg Beddis, and said, "Would you write all this down please, we are having a little bet".

"Sure", said Reg. "Sure" thinking it was just a bit of fun on a slow afternoon.

"Well", said Billy Boyd playing to the crowd. "How much do you wanna bet"?

"How about, how about", says Oliver steadying himself with the last of his rum. "How about my farm against yours".

"You can't be serious", responded Billy. "You must be mad".

"Not backing out now are you Billy Boyd"? responded Oliver sipping at his empty glass.

"Okay, if that's the way you want it. You're a mug, but I'll take your farm off you. If that's okay with you, Reg. Can you write this up for us"?

So the bet was duly written up in Reg's immaculate copper plate hand, witnessed and signed over a stamp.

"Right", said Billy. "That's that, what's everybody having, my shout unless any of you blighters want a side bet".

This caused roars of laughter as Oliver finished his pint and headed towards the door.

"What world class scrambler do you have lined up to make this fantastic ride"? asked Billy.

"I'm going to do it myself", said Oliver.

"What on that old Norton? You must be mad", said Billy.

"No. I'm gonna build a bike special like, just for you", which caused additional howls of laughter.

By this time I was getting fed upwith Billy Boyd chucking his new found wealth about. "Ok Billy Boy, I'll have a hundred on Oliver", I said.

"Same odds, thousand to one"? he nodded in reply.

"Good", I said. "Reg can add it to the contract".

As you leave the *Farmer's Arms* and turn down Walnut Avenue, you can just about see Oliver's place high on the far side of the valley, just below that bit of woodland south of Thorpe's Farm. And at night you could see Oliver's arc-welder sparking and flashing, lighting up the inside of his barn, but too far away to make out what he was up to. All I can say was that he was hard at it for weeks.

Now in those days, and you won't believe this, I had hair on my head, and lead in my pencil, and reckoned myself something of a ladies' man. Whether this was the cause of my marriage breaking down, or the result of it I couldn't say, but that's neither here nor there, and don't much matter. One Saturday afternoon Gloria Stokes and I had met up for a walk, all lovey-dovey, in the woods and one thing led to another, you know how these things go, and I shan't draw you a picture. Afterwards she gets the right hump, as they do sometimes, and storms off in tears. God help me. So I said to myself, "On Sh--. Well never mind", and all that, and I went for a walk all alone to reflect upon the inherent neurosis of the opposite sex. Later I found myself at Oliver's barn door where Oliver, with his back to me, was running a lathe. I didn't even know he had one.

"What ho, cousin", I says. "Long time no see, what have you been up to?"

The expression on his face, as he turned around, said murder or - at the very least - manslaughter or a good thump, but when he saw that it was me, his face softened a little. He knew that I would not gossip and would, if asked, keep my mouth firmly shut. However, my mouth must have hung open like a corpse when I saw what he had been working on all these long winter evenings.

I have never in all my life seen a motorcycle like it. It defied description, but I must try or this story will end right here that's for sure. It seems a shame to call it a motorbike at all, but it had a motor and two wheels, so I must.

The first thing I noticed was its rear wheel, off a tractor of course, and damn near as tall as I am. No suspension or shock absorbers and a frame made up of bent and welded scaffold poles. If the Forth Bridge had mated with an helicopter their offspring might reasonably be expected to look like this, having inherited its full share of its paternal Victorian rigidity and yet none of its mother's ethereal dragonfly grace. The engine was, he told me, a short block Ford V4 on top of which sat a Webber twin choke sports carburettor coupled to a turbo-charger from a diesel truck. The front forks were homemade, and the handlebars from his beloved Norton - sacrilege if you ask me – and the front tyre a knobbly motocross off-roader.

God alone knew what it would run like, but in any event it was a work of art. Cruel art, bitter art, art conceived in anger, hate and frustration, but art for all that. Hand painted in British Racing Green, it was topped off by a brightly polished fuel tank taken from an ATCO lawnmower with gleaming copper pipe work, which fed the thirsty carburettor. It must have weighed a ton or more, but you had to hand it to Oliver. It was a work of pure genius.

You are going to call me a cynic when I say that Oliver must have been on something to come up with this. He was big, he was slow, a regular dumb ox in anyone's estimation, and yet he had built - in just a few short months - this, this Leviathan which he called Caroline II. His way, I suppose, of working the pain she had left behind out of his system. He certainly looked healthier; his eyes were brighter and more alive. He had found for himself in the well of his loneliness, a purpose - unworthy as that purpose was - which was to bankrupt his chief tormentor. For if he won his bet, Billy Boyd would lose his farm and his life in the village would become intolerable. He would lose status and more; his self-respect in his own eyes if he, the great Billy Boyd tried to renege upon a bet made in public, written, signed and witnessed.

It was over a month before I encountered Oliver again. It was on the day of the contest. This time we were not alone, for the story of the impossible wager had spread far and wide, and there was a huge crowd assembled up by The Shield to see what would happen.

Mike was running a beer tent and a book on the event. Cash bets only and at more modest odds than Bill had rashly offered, I might add. There were vans selling burgers and hot dogs, others selling ice-cream, baked potatoes and candy floss. The lawyers for both Oliver and Bill were there to see fair play.

Billy was all smiles and overflowed with confidence. It had rained heavily overnight and the bog was a great deal boggier than a bog ought to be, unless it earnestly wished to be a lake; a fact which Billy continually tested from time to time with a long stick and tentative steps in his big Wellington boots to confirm that the bog could sustain no huge weight. It was just like a May Day fair. Even Caroline turned up on the back of the Harley, no doubt to chaff and scoff when her previous paramour came a cropper in the mud and the slime.

Just a little before noon, the sound of an un-silenced engine could be heard over and above the general din, and by degrees the crowd became hushed as all strained to hear. Louder and louder it became as it drew nearer and nearer. At the point at which it strained the eardrums, the monstrous motorcycle pulled into the field. A ripple of heat rose up from the un-silenced engine, bragging of its power and pride, and perfuming the air with the romantic stink of hot oil and metal.

Since I had seen it last, it had acquired chrome mudguards, a bank of spotlights, a windshield and a luxurious deep-buttoned tan leather king and queen pillion seat. It looked a proper treat.

If Oliver lost, I told myself, he could sell tickets just to look at the thing. To some eyes it was monstrous, ugly, evil even, but to others it was a marvel. It was a marvel that it moved at all. Lashed up out of odds and sods in a barn by an amateur engineer in just a few short months.

Oliver drew the monster up to within a few feet of the bog and as he sat there in his best all-purpose one and only, weddings and funerals suit, spotless white shirt, royal blue tie and polished boots, a diminutive figure in black leather stepped forward from the press of the crowd, her blonde hair bobbing in a delightfully coquettish manner.

"Hallo Oliver – have you missed me then?" It was Caroline.

"I think that it was ever so sweet of you to name your new motorcycle after me I mean, it shows that you still care for me, don't you"?

Oliver's eyes remained fixed upon the challenge before him.

"You going to give us a ride when you've won your bets? Why it will be just like old times, just you and me, and afterwards, if you want to, we might ---"

What they might have done afterwards I shall leave to your imagination, for just then he opened up the throttle and dropped the clutch. The big tractor tyre gripped the soft water-logged earth at the edge of the bog as the front wheel lifted just like a wild stallion in a movie, pawing the air. The bog, after weeks of rain, ought to have been more water than dirt, but the big tyre bit deep into it, raising a bow wave, and the motorcycle fairly ploughed its way over the surface. Instantly, its tread marks filled with water so that it seemed to be running on a grey silver chain. In less than 30 seconds it had crossed the so-called bottomless bog and paused on the lip of the fissure bank brisk with running water.

From where Oliver sat on his machine, he could have seen nothing of the ground beneath him, so steeply did it fall away. So it was the greatest leap of faith I have ever witnessed when he let in the clutch for the second time, and bike and rider toppled over the edge and disappeared from view. The crowd held its breath; he must fall, but no, that big bike rolled down the cliff face as slowly and steadily as a cable car, until a burst of revs told us that he had reached the flat and was opening her up for the run through the pool. Did I say pool? It might have been a puddle for all it mattered to Oliver. The Larkspur rocks, so much gravel, and the slippery clay might have been a wheelchair ramp.

Now comes the hard part, or so I thought, the return climb up the fissure which was, I might remind you, almost vertical and running with water as it trickled out from the bog. Oliver paused, and changed into his lowest gear, and with the engine roaring and the rear wheel slowly turning, the bike began to climb. The torque must have been enormous. For this stage Oliver lay flat over the tank with his boots on the rear footrests and off he went. One moment he was horizontal, next he was rising like a lift. Not quickly mark you, but resolute. I don't suppose that that big rear wheel lost its grip for an instant. Then he was up, and after a moment's precarious acrobatics, resumed his usual riding position and zipped across the bog once more. I reckoned that it was all about movement. As long as he kept moving there was no chance of his settling in the ooze.

The crowd cheered and clapped as he came to a halt. Bulbs flashed again and again, as journalists fought to get the best pictures for their papers. The two lawyers looked at each other and shrugged in amazement. Billy Boyd looked like a corpse. I have never seen a living face so drained of blood. I can never see a piece of veal without picturing Billy's face that afternoon.

"Oh Oliver, that was wonderful. I never did see anything like it. Take me back please Olly; I promise I won't ever leave you, not ever, not ever again!" Caroline looked up at him with big cow-like eyes. I believe she meant every word.

"You'll never leave me again?" said Oliver.

"No, never", said Caroline. "No my sweet big boy, we shall be together for always".

"Always together, together for always", said Oliver rubbing the talisman ATCO fuel tank. "Always Together Caroline and Oliver", said Oliver visibly trying to restrain the emotion in his voice as she climbed up behind him and settled into the deeply upholstered American-styled pillion seat.

With a whirr and a whoomph, the engine burst into life once again. Oliver opened the throttle, and once more the front wheel lifted from the ground. Flash bulbs popped again as the crowd cheered and whistled. One more time the big green motorcycle, with its chrome and polished metal, skimmed over the bog until ---.

Until, did I mention that to save weight Oliver had taken his petrol tank from an ATCO lawnmower? I did didn't I? It was brass and it was highly polished and very attractive there in the pale winter sunshine, but I doubt that it held more than half a gallon.

In the dead centre of the bog, the engine drank the last of it, coughed, spluttered, spat back through the carburettor and was still. Deathly still. To a man the spectators held their breath. Within a second, with the additional weight of a passenger, the big machine had sunk up to its hubs. Within 3 seconds it held them by the knees and had swallowed the engine completely. Then for some reason it slowed its rate of descent for a moment.

You would have expected Caroline to scream, for she was that sort of person as you know, much given to screeching and making a noise, but although her mouth was wide open no sound came. Shock – paralysis, who can say?

Oliver swivelled around on his seat and put his arm around her, and although it's rude to eavesdrop we all heard him say with more pure joy that I or anyone else for that matter had ever heard, "You'll never leave me again – together for always."

With that final vow, and a huge gaseous bubble, Oliver, Caroline I and Caroline II disappeared beneath the dark matrimonial blanket of the bog. Together for always and that was that.

The two lawyers shook hands and went home. The crowd dispersed and one by the police found duties to be attended to elsewhere. Mike said all small bets were off, and Billy Boyd found a new lease of life, and stood round after round of drinks at the bar at the *Farmer's Arms*.

"What are you having, Jimbo?" he said as I walked up to the bar.

"That's very nice of you," I replied. "Let's see, a hundred pounds at a thousand to one. That works out at a hundred thousand pounds you owe me for starters."

"Sorry Jimbo, all bets are off – ask Mike," he says looking smug.

"Bets maybe, but this was a contract. It was your idea to have solicitor Reg Beddis write it up right here in this very bar. A deed no less. The contract provided for an entertainment. If it was performed the price was your farm. If he failed to deliver he lost his farm in penalty. Our bet was not a wager but a management fee. All perfectly legal, ask your solicitor. You saw him shake hands with Reg Beddis this afternoon. So Billy Boy, I'll have a cheque from you for one hundred grand tomorrow morning, and the deeds to your farm as soon as possible, say by the end of the month."

"My farm?" he stuttered. "What the bloody hell has my farm got to do with you?"

"Well, you lost it to Oliver, and Oliver's dead. So it passes to his next of kin. That's me, he was my cousin. I thought you knew that. I thought everybody knew that."

Billy's face might have been carved out of chalk. I was enjoying this immensely.

"Well, as you are in the chair I think I will have that drink. This calls for champagne. Anyone care to join me in a farewell toast to Oliver?"

# GRASS

B ack in the good old days before computers, CCTV cameras and DNA profiling; before the Police & Criminal Evidence Act (1984 ) when the victim still had more rights than the accused, the good old British Bobby had a couple of time-tested weapons at his disposal to assist him in his fight to keep the streets clean and safe, and to nudge his career a notch or two up the ladder of advancement. Namely fitting up and grassing.

If you recall Jesus Christ was grassed up by one of his mates Judas Iscariot and even before then there was Joseph's brothers tampering with the evidence. Then whilst his head was still ringing with that indignity Potiphar's randy wife Zuleikha had him slung into chokey on a bogus charge of rape as a reward for his rectitude.

Not that Joseph was above a bit of fitting up on his own account. Remember, the silver cup WAS found in Benjamin's sack.

But I digress. Suffice it to say that such practices have been around for a very long time.

One officer of my acquaintance had this business down to such a fine art that with some justification you might call it a science, and being the professional that he undoubtedly was had risen in the ranks accordingly.

P.C. William Oldswell had risen to the rank of sergeant and then inspector of The Metropolitan Police's CID Department purely on his arrest record, which was second to none, for he barely scraped through his promotion examinations.

The various commanders, and chief's superintendent who sat on his promotion boards liked him from the outset. He was a no nonsense down to earth copper who revelled in the business of nicking villains. He wouldn't admit this but he would often stand before the long hall mirror at home and practice saying, "You're nicked chummie, get your coat," or, "Now don't do anything silly", or with a cool emphasis, "cuff him sergeant".

"I am an old fashioned thief taker gentlemen," he delighted to say to the assembled gold braid, "No more, no less." And they loved him for it.

"He", they would say amongst themselves, "is the backbone of the force." That was not to say that he would ever make chief inspector, much less superintendent. After all there are limits to good will, and patronage must ever be constrained by common sense.

Still he was not to know that, and as the years ticked by worked ever harder to achieve that unattainable goal.

"Nick the bastards, lock 'em up. They're all scum." He got a special little frisson of pleasure in banging up the black ones but by and large he didn't care; it was the result that mattered. Black or white, it was another notch on the metaphorical truncheon. Not that he knew a metaphor from a pound of tea. He had a system and that system worked a treat.

Although in essence his system was simple, it required constant observation and assiduous attention to detail, a cross-reference filing system and scrupulous methods.

In his day to day dealings with the criminal classes he was constantly on the look out for those unconsidered trifles and daily discards, the collection of which formed the nexus of his system. Beer cans, cigarette packets, toffee wrappers, even bits of chewing gum. In fact, anything known to have been touched by a suspect. You have to realise that the professional villain wouldn't dream of ever leaving his prints at the scene of a crime. Only mugs get careless. But outside, in the pub or in the supermarket we leave our fingerprints all over the place.

No collector of stamps or butterflies was ever more painstaking in the gathering and classifying of a collection than he.

The box room of his Orpington semi contained just that - boxes.

Hundreds of them, large and small, all numbered and colour-coded. On the one wall not hidden behind white melamine shelving, were his wall charts - showing who was inside and who wasn't. Who was due out and when, and who was ripe for a pull. Then the top ten - the list of those who ought to be put back inside as soon as possible. There upon these shelves, waiting for their turn in the judicial spotlight, sat the silent witnesses to crimes yet to happen.

In those days everyone on division knew who was "At it", that is to say engaged in professional criminal activities. So if there were no obvious suspects for a particular job, nobody spending cash like a sailor, nobody flogging knocked off goods round the pubs, then the Oldswell system came into its own . Out shot the long arm of the law to pull in anyone who looked a bit of a likely lad.

And if said lad was not having tea with the vicar, his MP, his probation officer or ladies of the WI at the time in question or had some other cast iron alibi, then said lad was deep in the malodorous ooo'nasty.

After an hour or so in the interview room DI Oldswell would tire of hearing the same old mantra. "I didn't do it, I wasn't there, I want my solicitor", and switch off the tape recorder and send the looming constable by the door out for teas. Cigarettes would appear and the DI would lean back and say "Look here Johnny. I know you didn't do it. You know you didn't do it, so let's stop pissing about shall we? I think you know who did pull it. Your lot are as thick as thieves down the Wallworth Road so let's see what's going t happen after I've had a nice cup of tea in your pleasant company. The Scenes of Crime Officer and I are going to pay another visit to the scene of the crime and do you know what I am going to find there, with your dabs all over it? No. Well let me look in my little red book and see what's on offer. Crisp packet. Nice smooth surface, get some lovely prints off of that. No, What about a Curly Wurly wrapper? You like those don't you? How about a book of matches from The Bongo-a-go-go Club? Not a member are you by any chance? Yes, I thought you might be . Book of matches it is then. Easy to see how we missed something small like that on our first visit.

"So, Johnny are you going to help me with my enquiries and point the finger at the real villain or go down for a stiff five? Oh no, I was forgetting, silly me. It will be seven with your record and you with a baby on the way too, such a shame. Never see his daddy .

"What will Brenda say? Nothing I expect, probably find another bloke. Lots of young fit black bucks on your estate these days. What is it about blondes they find so attractive when they have got some lovely girls of their own? Turns my stomach just to imagine it. How about you? Have you thought of a name for the baby yet? What about Winston? Very popular name these days in your part of the manor."

What sort of choice is that for a man, grass up a fellow professional or do the time for him?

Credit where credit is due, DI Oldswell never asked anybody to stand up in court, just point the finger. If the perpetrator's flat was not over-flowing with evidence he was sure to be able to provide some of his own to bridge that particular lacuna. Even if Johnny slipped out of the net this time by grassing up a pal, there was always the risk that Oldswell, if he so chose, could grass up the grass, with dire life-changing consequences.

Within a year or so of his retirement, something happened, just off Peckham High Street which rocked DI Oldswell's world to the core. The Armstrong Cash & Carry was done over by a couple of lads during the hours of darkness. They had to be young and fit to climb up onto the roof, force an entry and slide down a rope into the cashier's office, and make their escape by the same route with the contents of the safe and sacks full of irresistible loot; whisky, tobacco, sweets and the like.

The young man the DI pulled in for this offence was Wayne Barnabus, a shelf-stacker from Tesco's Supermarket. He had had his eye on young Wayne for some time. A clean sheet thus far, but that would change. After all he was the nephew of Barry Barnabus, well known Peterman currently taking a sabbatical in Wormwood Scrubs.

Wayne was a pleasant young man and as innocent as it is possible to be living, drinking and working in any of the South London Villages collectively known as "M" division.

In his archive refrigerator DI Oldswell had a half-eaten Mars bar, which had once been owned and bitten into by Wayne. What more evidence could a jury want if found at the scene of the crime, particularly as boxes of Mars bars had been taken in the raid?

Nonplussed by the whole turn of events Wayne was told, in no uncertain terms that by the time the white coated lads at the MPD lab had done their stuff and matched up his finger prints and his teeth marks, he could expect a fair old stretch behind stout walls at her majesty's expense. Unless.... Unless, of course he was ready to play ball, and finger the young tearaways of his acquaintance from whom he had purchased, only yesterday, a catering sized tin of Maxwell House and a 10kg tub of butter for his old gran.

Not an easy choice for an 18 year old soon to take his driving test. But realising that there could be but one outcome resulting from his silence, he accepted the *fait accompli* and delivered the two lambs to the slaughter.

Within hours these two novice villains were caught red-handed with a transit van full of good stuff which had been pulled over ostensibly for a faulty brake light whilst on their way to East Lane Market, where their Uncle Rupert had his café.

I will not go so far as to say that young Wayne had any objection on moral grounds to such treatment, in South London morals don't start until you reach Croydon - Purley even.

Neither was he over-concerned that the Johnson Brothers might find out that it was he who had grassed them up, even thought it might result, should they ever find out, in his wearing his foreskin as a hat. It was, and these are my words not his, the atavistic feeling of injustice which sat heavily on his young mind. It was also, I would conjecture, his wounded pride and the blow to his self-respect that hurt most. Between stacking up the tubs of ice cream and restocking the frozen fish fingers, he began to plan his revenge, which as you know is a dish best served cold. A plan which sprouted, grew, flourished and fruited with an abundance he could never have imagined.

Mrs Detective Inspector Oldswell, Maureen to her friends, was a rather ordinary woman, typical of her time and class. She had her hair done once a fortnight, cooked a roast on Sundays, ironed her husband's shirts and took his suits to the cleaners -fingerprint powder can make such a mess. In short, a domestic goddess. Attractive too, well once upon a time perhaps, and as the flowers of her charm faded and gravity levied its inevitable tax upon a woman's body so too did her sexual appetite become a thing of fond, if overrated memory.

Day by day her flock house coat and worn slippers became less resistible as clothing of choice. To be fair, she did her best to fight her descent into bored sluttishness even though her employment of Plymouth Gin as an assistant was not the best choice of confederate she might have selected. The pencil marks she made upon its label out of feelings of guilt stood as a rough and ready barometer of the progress of this campaign,

Like a spy on a mission, Wayne kept watch upon his target and from a safe distance kept a note of the routines of the Oldswell household, and of those little signals which pass between long-married folk. After a week of this Wayne deduced, quite correctly, that a degree of friction existed between the Oldswells and he would be buggered if he did not have enough puff in his young lungs to turn a spark into an inferno.

Knowing that Mrs O' took his suits to the cleaners on a Saturday morning it was but the work of a moment for Betty, Wayne's girlfriend, to slip a packet of condoms into the inspector's pocket with one missing. They were specialist items too. Multi- coloured, lubricated and contoured for maximum pleasure. Maureen had never heard of such things, much less seen one or, heaven forbid, handled one.

That night the Inspector went home to a very frosty house. Not that he cared above half. Time of life, he told himself. He, like a good husband, had prepared his mind in advance for the onset of hot flushes and mood swings. Best not rise to the bait eh, least said. Say no more.

War had been declared and the first shots had been fired in anger. Over the next week there were a series of curious phone calls. If he answered the phone the caller spoke gibberish.

"Hello inspector. She's naked, but it's all right down at the station. The superintendent says two teas and a pickled egg. Last Thursday or next Tuesday. Yes are you going to charge them yet? The gelignite is in the pigeon loft. The Irish are bringing it in, in a coat hanger, code shoe horn do you understand me? Yes, inspector big job Saturday. Is Maureen there? The big fellow has the guns". And so it went on. The longer he went on listening to this rubbish, the less likely his wife would be to believe it was rubbish or a crossed line. If she should pick up the phone first there would be a long silence or a muted sob before the caller hung up.

About a week later the first of the plain paper packaged books arrived. She opened it. She opened all their mail. She burnt it in the living room grate of course, but what she couldn't burn were the images which were seared on her mind. How could people do such things? She shivered. The gin barometer fell a good few degrees that morning. She steeled herself for worse to come and continued to open their mail. What was this? Two tickets to see Evita. If they were for his mistress why have them sent here? She would be cool about this. That would frustrate whatever little game he was playing. She placed the tickets on the mantelpiece behind the clock where he could not fail to see them. Let him bluff his way out of this one. As it happened he didn't try. He thought that she had brought them and left it at that.

But he hadn't sent them had he? Wayne had. Why? To have them out of the house at the same time of course.

All things considered, their trip up west had been pleasant enough. Suspicions on hold for the moment. They had a drink in *The Coach* on Berwick Street and a passable steak in a Berni Inn near Trafalgar Square.

Neither imagining the unexploded bomb awaiting them at home.

As Wayne knew from his observations, the inspector would garage the car as she went in to put the kettle on.

The little red light was flashing on the answer phone, and all unsuspecting she picked up the handset and pressed play.

"Have you told her yet?" A pause. "Please Billy you promised that you would tell her tonight, after the show. Make it easy for the old cow you said."

Betty delivered the short soliloquy with all the emotion and polish of a professional fresh from the Oscars.

If the first pause was long and the second pause longer, the third pause was, as they say, pregnant.

"It didn't come yet and I've always been so regular. Call me soon Billy. Miss Mouse misses her Mr Truncheon".

The blood drained from her face, first with embarrassment, then with a sudden change of mood turned bright red with anger. As she slammed the phone down with a crash which sent shattered pieces of black plastic in all directions, the inspector, whistling "Don't Cry for Me Argentina", walked through the front door and into a hurricane.

"You bastard. Who is she?" Spite and venom were in every syllable.

"Who? Who, what are you on about woman? She who? I don't know who you mean."

Which was true, he didn't.

"Don't lie to me you bastard. All those phone calls. Late shifts. Special investigations. Well now we know."

"Know what woman - have you gone stark raving bonkers?"

"Mad am I? We shall see who's bloody mad and who isn't. Now get out of my home before I kill you."

That night he dossed down at the station. Not in a cell, but perhaps he should have for it suited the mood of the moment better.

Eight hours restless sleep had incubated the poison nicely and her first call of the day was to the editor of the *News of The World*, who in turn telephoned the Commissioner of Police for the Metropolis.

The Headlines said it all

## ANONYMOUS GRASS BLOWS WHISTLE ON BENT COP
## DOZENS WRONGLY CONVICTED
## DEN OF FABRICATED EVIDENCE FOUND IN INSPECTOR'S HOME

The cost of retrials and compensations ran into millions. Oldswell lost his job and his pension, and after a swift trial received five years in prison, reduced to three for good behaviour, all of which he spent wondering who on earth had set up the whole thing. He never did find out.

Well, he is out now and the irony is this. It was Wayne Barnabus, promoted to manager, who gave him a job. Not much of a job it is true - picking up unconsidered trifles and daily discards, keeping the supermarket car park neat and tidy. You know the sort of things that people leave behind. Beer cans, cigarette cartons, toffee wrappers, crisp packets, and every now and again a half eaten Mars bar, but he never, ever, takes any of it home.

# NOT A HAPPY MAN

Y ou had to know him rather well to understand that Hubert Templeton was not a happy man. For his happiness, or rather lack of it, was a status which was neither tacit nor manifest considering his material situation, which was excellent by the way.

There were signs though, plenty of them if you cared to look, but few people did. Either, I would imagine, because they lacked the necessary interpersonal skills or, as is more likely, because they felt that his woes were not their woes and best left undisturbed. People can be like that as you know.

Had anyone the temerity to ask if he were happy he would have responded quickly enough, perhaps with a dismissive wave of the hand saying something to the effect that as he saw it happiness was an insubstantial and relative concept, and that he preferred to deal in certainties. An answer which might fob off the curious, but not someone with the incisive sensitivity to see the desperately dark storm lines of deep trouble building up on his mental horizon.

Admit it or not, it was a question which had occupied much of his time of late, and if he were as scrupulously honest with himself as he believed himself to be, it was one which had always perplexed him in one guise or another for as long as he could recall. While we are being frank with one another, who has not sought to grasp the unravelling thread of destiny and dowse out its meaning, if indeed life has a meaning?

From the perspective of his elevated affluence he concluded that without some sort of meaning, however obscure, life was - in fact - pointless. Pointless perhaps, but not profitless, for he had built up, starting with nothing, a vast commercial undertaking and amassed a considerable fortune with homes in London, Paris, San Francisco and the Bahamas.

This night he sat in his great leather armchair before a roaring and crisply crackling log fire. Stretched out in his thin silk-trousered legs, he wriggled his old toes in his soft calf leather slippers and reached nonchalantly for a long necked crystal decanter, from which he poured himself a generous measure of fine old crusty port into a paper thin glass. One of a set which had been engraved, at a whim, by the master engraver Le Mat with his personal; motto "Dare to venture" - a very free translation of a poem by Ben Side, a 12th Century Syrian poet which runs, if my memory serves me right, "Dare you venture to embrace death before death embraces you" - an impeachment to the world-weary no doubt to put up or shut up. Hubert was not a religious man, but nevertheless he still wondered what punishment, if any, awaited such a pre-emptive embrace. Casting aside the priceless gift of life in the ultimate gesture of ingratitude.

Warm, seated beside his own fireside deep in contemplation, his mind crossed many borders and decades. Between the high tide of nostalgia and the low tide of a cruel solitude he could, at the ebb of circumstances, stand back a little and in the fulsome light of reason's day say, without equivocation, that his life, when rolled out scroll-like, was not a happy one. For it was only in moments like these he reflected that he was able to formulate an honest and manly appreciation of his half-century or so here upon earth.

Don't get me wrong in this for there were many bright, some might say brilliant, moments in his life. Brightness which some less fortunate in business or love might have cause to envy. But with a sigh and another glass of port he could see, as no other could, that they were no more than the sort of sparks which, borne aloft from the heart of a spiteful fire, soared upwards to extinction in the darkness of a tall and seemingly endless chimney.

There were many people in those days who, viewing his elegant apartment, with its central location and fine comfortable old furniture, his paintings, his powerful car and his apparently endless resources, would have gladly changed places with him.

Oh! How he wished someone would. Oh! For a week or a year to be a simple clerk, a driver or postman. To draw his pay on Friday and stop off for a pint of ale on his way home to a stout and comfortable wife. There to be the adored idol of a couple of very average children who had waited lovingly looking at the kitchen clock for the time when daddy would arrive. Tired but never too tired to play games before supper.

He could, with a measure of malt whisky inside him, sustain this little self-deception for quite extended periods of time. Digging the allotment by the railway line on a Saturday morning, supporting the lads in the afternoon "Come on you Lions". Laying lino in the hall, or creosoting the fence. Ah yes, but … but even then he would have to admit that as postman or clerk he was too intellectually arrogant to accept such a situation for very long, and then the idyll would crumple, until the next time.

He could no more have sat down to an evening of television quiz shows or popular soap operas than he could have cut off his own thumbs with blunt pliers. These thoughts, and so very much more, ran before his mind's eye. Like the time in '69 and again in '81 when he ….. but no! Let's not go there with him. Some other time perhaps, for it is quite a story, but not now. Not when other things hang in the balance.

His grandfather's service pistol sat like a small self-contained demon upon the highly polished table adjacent to the almost empty decanter, and he glanced at it from time to time in an off-hand manner, as if the time for contemplation had not completely passed, though the magnetism it held for his eyes was undiminished.

He had taken it from its case that very morning and lightly oiled its mechanism. It worked perfectly, though slaughter was but a memory to it for it had not spoken in anger for almost a century.

With steadier hands than you would believe possible he slipped a single vintage cartridge between the lips of the magazine, and with great care worked the slide back between thumb and forefinger and watched as the round fed smoothly into the chamber, where it lay patiently waiting. Gently he lowered the hammer and engaged the little safety lever with a snick. He returned it to the table where it now sat poised like a silent black cobra. "Call me", it seemed to whisper in hushed and reverential tones. "Breathe my name in the valley of shadowy thoughts and I shall be instantly alive to your commands and ready to strike at your bidding. For I give strength to the weak and courage to the fearful. Move but a finger and I shall open my hot throat and sing you a song of release like no other".

These things it whispered but just for now it lay still, its sinister beauty softly reflected in the highly polished rosewood.

One must ask, what remains for a brave man when his day's portion of faith in himself runs dry and he discovers that all his hopes of a happier tomorrow have absconded? Courage and/or anger may fill the gap, but not forever and what happens thereafter? I cannot say, for I do not know. Perhaps there are no answers.

High on the ornate marble mantelpiece, a splendid gilt and ebony clock softly nibbled at the remaining moments of his life. He downed the last of the port and lit a cigar, his first for a decade, but even though it was Cuban and of premier quality it tasted foul. He cast it into the fire. A biblical connotation surfaced in his mind, and with equal suddenness, escaped him. In a single swift continuous motion he picked up the pistol, flicked off the safety catch, re-cocked the hammer, placed the muzzle to his ear and swiftly pulled the trigger.

The internal mechanism of this robust pistol worked all too well. The hammer released from its retaining sear, flew forward in a little arc to strike the hardened steel firing pin. In its turn the pin buried its head deep into the copper cap which contained a few grains of fulminate. This volatile composition held its breath in guilty defiance at this conspiracy to self-murder and failed to ignite the main charge of nitro-cellulose. Perhaps excusing its disobedience on the grounds of senility owing to its great age..

I am sure that you will agree with me, even without personal experience, that the sheer relief which follows a failed suicide attempt has to be without parallel in the lexicon of human emotional expression. For instead of the expected lethal thunderclap he heard nothing save the crisp metallic click of the falling hammer followed by a profound silence.

Discounting his long considered resolve and his earnest determination to sidestep the existential burden, which had hung albatross-like around his neck, since, well since forever, and in spite of his low self-esteem, itself a paradox in a self-made millionaire. In spite also of a long history of love's offerings held in contempt and flung time after time into the gutter before his very eyes. In spite of passions spurned and need decried, fate had intervened in his life on the side of the angels for once, and some nameless, shapeless demon had scuttled aside, all fear, bitterness and disillusion defeated. Cheated of its victory at the eleventh hour. His grand gesture of God defiance had turned to ashes in his hand . Who could say, perhaps his arrogant worthless life had turned a corner and it was a released caged bird that he could now hear singing and fluttering in his breast..

But God and fate and destiny could wait upon the sunrise. It was sufficient, more than sufficient now to be alive, gloriously alive. Notwithstanding that his world had turned upside down, leaving his head spinning. There was so much he must re-examine, but not now, now was not the time. He would take his new found tranche of emotions to bed.

He replaced the pistol upon the table gently, as if he owed it something. Feeling suddenly exhausted and drained as he rose unsteadily to his feet, sleep and the eiderdown of dreams called to him now. Tomorrow he would square up to life and view the world with fresh eyes. His hands were trembling. Perhaps a nightcap would steady his nerves. Forgetting that he had already drunk almost a whole bottle of port, he reached for the depleted decanter.

I can only suppose that the pretty rosewood table shook a little as he grasped the decanter. For something, some slight movement perhaps had served to remind the old military cartridge of its duty for it awoke from its 100 year siesta with a crash that sent the massive .45 calibre bullet racing for its freedom up the short barrel to emerge rather full of itself, replete with purposeful velocity, ebullience, hunger and mischief.

First it bit off a piece of the piecrust edge of the little table. Then it flew across the room like a mad hornet passing effortlessly through a Ming vase, which - unaccustomed to such barbarity - collapsed from the shock. It reconsidered its flight plan upon introducing itself to an unbelievably rare Rodin bronze, ricocheting upwards at about 60 degrees, losing a little of its earnest alacrity perhaps, but none of its resolve for it had reserved sufficient aggression to splinter the walnut case and irreplaceable mechanism of an 18th Century long case clock accredited to the master horologist Thomas Tompion, sending a ragged splinter through a small but rather exquisite Renoir on the adjacent wall.

It would be reasonable were you to suppose that the euphoria of being alive had never before been known to evaporate so quickly as many hundreds of thousands of pounds worth of antiquities lay ruined all around him. All uninsured of course. What need has a nascent suicide of contents insurance. I will leave it to your excellent imagination to picture the exact shade of purple pigment which now coloured the palette of his misery.

His jaw dropped as a tsunami of dark thoughts swept over him, compared with which his earlier morbid preoccupations had been but an unwelcome shower.

But as I have said, for all his wealth Hubert Templeton was never a happy man.

# PEACHY

To return to the peacetime army after a costly and bloody war is considered by many professionals as a return to proper soldiering. Field exercises, parades and bullshine. If you have ever served in the forces you must admit that as an institution it has much to commend it. Senior officers court the local gentry with at least half an eye to political advancement. Junior officers set off in quest of a means of promotion less predicated to pain and mutilation. NCOs focus their minds on avoiding trouble, working the system whilst simultaneously feathering their nests with as much cash and creature comforts as can be had by the application of intrepid valour and marshal audacity. In this they are assisted by several generals. General apathy, general neglect, general decay, wear and tear. From quartermaster sergeant to corporal cook they all have a finger in the proverbial pudding.

Whilst all this is in progress the private soldier is left to fight the greatest enemy of all. Boredom. This he does as he has always done since first armies ever were, the essential principals of which are written in every soldier's pay book. One, eat and sleep wherever possible. Two, drink and fornicate wherever and whenever possible. Three, keep your trap shut and remember it's us against them. Thus the esprit de corps of an army is maintained and on the whole, by and large, it works rather well. Better than being constantly dirty, wet, hungry, shot at and abused anyway.

Having said that it was not the state of affairs welcomed by everyone.

Colonel Hiram Peach was just such a malcontent. He was, or so he believed, a fighting soldier from a long line of fighting soldiers. His father had fought under Pershing. His grandfather had ridden boot to boot with Teddy Roosevelt Roughriders in Cuba. Both illustrious ancestors had retired as Generals.

Much to his disappointment, Pugnacious Peach had spent the war years assiduously guarding America's vital infrastructure, such as it was of interest to enemy aliens in the state of Georgia. Ambition infused his erect military frame like the mint in a mint julip. If he did not achieve general rank before he retired, preferably in a goddamn shooting war, then he was going to die in the attempt for that was the sort of man he was. General Mark Fishbinder was on the prowl and could spring an inspection at any moment. Today could be the day. Colonel Peach was resolved to kick ass up and down the pay grades until there was not a speck of dust

---

out of place in the whole of Fort Peach.

"Jesus Christ Mary," he said as he tied his silk olive green tie, speaking to his wife's reflection in the mirror. "It's gonna be another hot one".

"My my Peachy, I do wish that you would refrain from using the Lord's name in such a profane and improper manner," she replied disapprovingly in a soft Gone with the Wind southern drawl, the likes of which still exists in the nostalgic confederacy between the lower upper classes and the upper lower classes of the deep south.

"Well it sure is hot, close too. I reckon the humidity must be 90% at least and it's early yet." He fingered his starched collar uneasily and pulled on his gun belt.

No ordinary gun belt. This, in fact, was his unique side arm; an expertly customised and aesthetically horrendous sawn off 1880's vintage 12 gauge double-barrelled shotgun, made originally for an English earl by Purdy's of London. The old gunsmith, Atlanta's best, who effected the barbaric truncation actually had tears in his eyes as his zip saw bit into the venerable damascene steel barrels. Still business is business.

With something like, but not quite, reverence, Colonel Peach slid the gun into its hand stitched chrome leather holster; his fingers lingering just a second or so on the butt, which was polished to new horse chestnut brightness. A great weapon for clearing a speak-easy of hoodlums, but utterly useless in any challenge involving tanks. Unless of course, one was of an anachronistic crusading quixotic turn of mind which Hiram Peach was, of course. "I swear that it gets heavier every day Mary," he said snapping the silver buckle into place.

"I don't see why you bother, Hiram. It's not as if Mr Khrushchev himself is going to drop in by parachute."

"Hmm, I don't see why not, Rudolph Hess did just that. Still if General Patton could tote his pearl handled six guns, then I just gotta carry this baby. It's my trademark you might say. The men know who I am at a glance and the top brass can't help but notice. Who's that? Why that's Pug Peach, Mr President."

"That's the boy for me. Set him on the commie bastards and the cold war will be over in a week, yes Sir."

He gave his turnout a final once over in the large cheval mirror that had once belonged to his hero General Robert E. Lee, or so he believed. From his close cropped hair to his gleaming cavalry boots he was every inch a soldier's soldier. Only one thing, small in itself, spoiled this splendid image. Colonel Peach suffered from an annoying facial tic. More pronounced when under stress, but could twitch embarrassingly at almost any time. He had some pills which helped of course, that is when he could remember to take them. Which, to be honest, wasn't often. But then most days he had little to worry about unduly.

"Have a nice day, Peachy," his wife said as he turned into the hall. "And don't forget your pills."

"In blue blazes, Mary, I wish you would stop calling me that, you know it annoys the hell out of me. If it wasn't bad enough that some wag in the Pentagon posted me here, Colonel Peach, Fort Peach, Peach County, Georgia." He paused and drew a deep breath.

"I swear some of my officers have started calling me that behind my back." His voice was calm and controlled but it was impossible for him to totally hide his rising tide of anger.

"And another thing, General Fishbinder could drop in at any time now. Please, Mary just for me, please try to stay sober, just this once. Take the car, have your hair done. Wear that pretty organdie dress why don't you?"

She made no reply. Perhaps she hadn't heard him. Still it riled him. Had he heard, or had he imagined the clink of ice dropping into a glass. Turning on his heel he marched out of the house. The little bottle of pills that he had forgotten to remember sitting in silent witness to his mood on the hallstand.

In spite of its Commanding Officer's cavalry boots, Fort Peach Georgia was an infantry establishment. Most of its rank and file soldiers were Afro-Americans as we say nowadays. Negroes as they would have said then. The officer corps were exclusively white, and Yankees to boot from way north of the Mason-Dixon line, but that's by the by.

As in any culture riven into parts by virtue of class or race, alternative hierarchies develop. A mirror image you might say wherein a legislature of sorts makes the rules and an executive of sorts enforces them. With alternative doctors and alternative chemists dispensing such uppers and downers as free enterprise demands.

Twin brothers, privates Elijah and Joshua, alike as two niblets on a corn cob, were, it might be said, well placed and highly respected in this world of shades and shadows, for without question they were masters of the esoteric art in which they excelled, practised in secret, and were lauded in public. It was an art practised by many in the South but perfected by very few. These boys, for they were just boys when all was said and done, could take discarded, bruised, split and rotten fruit and in a dark enclave between two Quonset huts transmute so much trash into gold. Peach brandy in other words. To call it moonshine would be to flatter the moon and to insult these alchemists. For whilst the inspirational light of the moon might warm a heart lost in the glaciers of time it could not, even with the largest burning glass, light the fires that their wonderful brandy could. Do you know, I can even taste it now. Ah - I have a dream. But enough of that.

As his daily round continued, Colonel Peach began to feel a little easier in his mind, if not body, as the brassy sun rose in the royal blue sky. With a silvery silent click the thermometer ratcheted up another degree, and with an appropriately empathetic squelch the humidity graph followed suit. In true synchronous harmony the Colonel's blood pressure did likewise.

As a slight, very slight, panacea to his discomfort, Colonel Peach noted with pleasure that the pots and pans in the cookhouse gleamed as they should. There were no men's magazines in the guard room. No cigarette butts in the orderly office, no private cars in the motor pool awaiting tune ups, and in the armoury there were no embarrassing gaps in the rows of stacked arms. The whole camp smelled delightfully military. The aroma of fresh paint and metal polish offset by the all pervading smell from the nearby peach orchards. General Fishbinder - Ha! Let him come, for what had he to worry about? Nothing that's what. He ran a tight ship that other Commanding Officers might well use as an example to their credit. It was then that he saw, at a distance, a cloud on the horizon of this paradigm of military efficiency through the heat haze of this laundry hot forenoon.

Across the camp, Elijah and Joshua were coming to the end of a fresh batch of 50 gallons of their premier product. An open secret amongst the rank and file, the small, compact and well-concealed distillery sat wedged between cookhouse number one and the regimental store of World War I vintage bicycles. Its location had much to recommend it, from a tactical perspective that is, but with the heat and fumes so generated, working in such a small space would take their toll and stepping out as the brothers did into the fresh air the effect is like a kick from a cow giraffe.

With shirts hanging out and unbuttoned uniforms awry and legs like India rubber, the boys emerged from the secret entrance to their still room and steered a ragged course back to their hut. They may have been singing Swanee, but the evidence is a little uncertain. From way across the parade ground Colonel Peach's eagle eye took this in. Keyed up as he was to look for the slightest infringement of military discipline a general inspection being imminent.

"Sergeant Major Schlumberger"

"Sir"

"Sergeant Major, those men, over there, are drunk. By God if they are then they shall pay for this. It's not even noon yet. Damn reds."

"Reds Sir?"

"Reds, communists, fifth columnists."

"Oh yes Sir - communists, but er I don't think…"

"Don't think, follow me. I'll, I'll."

He might have said more, and expanded upon his interpretation of ideological systems, but his facial tic or spasm had started up. He had forgotten to take his daily dose of Tegretol, a strong nerve suppressant.

Like a rolling roadblock composed of two Sherman tanks, he and the Sergeant Major came to a crisp halt across the path of twins Elijah and Joshua Polk who, although high as kites on brandy fumes, nevertheless came to an instant stop. Erect if still swaying.

"Oh ho, you men, you men, you're drunk, stinking drunk and it's the stockade for you as sure as my name is …"

In that second, that very second, the cogs of the alternative society slipped with lubricated synchromesh into action. A crowd of olive green clad infantry men formed about them. A micro-second later voices from the back of the throng could be heard raised in anger.

"Yo bitch mother be goddamn washerwoman."

"Yo hush your mouth nigger."

"No frigging cotton picking field han gonna call me nigger!"

With that the ruckus started in earnest and the noise level rose as the crowd picked its champions and took sides with cries of "whoa buck" and "sic him blood."

"What the hell now. Today of all days," said the Colonel as he turned to see what was going on not fifteen feet behind him. The Sergeant Major was scanning faces and noting names.

As they looked away, many hands, rough but protective, dragged Elijah and Joshua back into the crowd where they were instantly submerged in a sea of black faces. Other hands with equal insistence pushed two other men, two other stone cold sober men; into their place. This being Georgia it will excite no remark to mention that these two were also brothers, also twins. William and Wilberforce Watt. But whereas Elijah and Joshua were identical, as identical as two freshly washed beer bottles, Bill and Will were as different as maybe. No sooner had the Colonel and his senior NCO turned towards the noise than the ruckus abruptly ended and a deathly hush prevailed overall. The whole distracting episode had lasted not three seconds. Turning back to the matter in hand the Colonel's jaw dropped. One suspect was now 6ft 3ins whilst the other a little over 5ft 8ins.

"What!" exclaimed the Colonel.

"Sir …" both men said in sober unison.

Although he was not one of those white officers to whom all blacks look the same, neither was he of the old school who could pick out a man of Yoruba or Mandinga descent from facial type alone but he could see something was not quite right and with the sun nearing its peak in the heavens he began to perspire and his face began to tic.

"You're drunk the pair of you!" he said with great emphasis. "What do you have to say for yourselves?"

The taller one, William, answered for them both, trying his darndest to suppress a small but persistent speech impediment which appeared whenever he was flustered.

"I da da doan wish to contra-dict the Colonel Sir but wez never drinks cosen wez ba ba ba ba Baptists Sir."

The Colonel leaned forward towards Wilberforce until his face was barely an inch away from the private's face hoping to catch a whiff of alcohol upon his breath.

The nervous disposition shared by the twins, and the root cause of William's stutter, manifested itself in Wilberforce as a facial tic not unlike that possessed by the Colonel, except that whereas his was on the left cheek the Colonel's was on the right.

The Colonel's face twitched, closely followed by an echoing twitch from Wilberforce. To the Colonel it must have seemed like looking in a mirror that had suddenly become a photographic negative. They twitched again in time on this occasion.

"See that Sergeant Major? That's insolence. He's mocking me. The bastard thinks he can mock me today; today of all days with the General about to ..."

He stepped back a pace.

"Oh, so you think it's funny do you? Well I'll teach you to mock a senior officer."

"No Sir, not mocking, not you Sir. Was I?" he said turning to his brother.

"No Sir not m - m - m - mocking, not you Sir, we respects you c - c - c - Colonel."

Then by virtue of nothing greater than the sympathetic magic that exists between twins, he started to twitch too. For the first time in his life at that.

"By God this is too much Sergeant Major," said the Colonel, one sweaty palm resting on the butt of his unusual side arm.

"Sir," said the Sergeant.

With cheek ticking and blood pressure rising, the Colonel began to turn an angry red and the veins at his temples began to pulse and to pound like apache war drums.

The sun shone down and the humidity rose, greedily sucking moisture from the red Georgia clay as if Georgia itself wanted to take this Yankee officer down a peg or two.

"Right, mock me, mock your country's uniform. I'll see to it that you will be digging ditches for the rest of your time in this man's army. Do you understand me?"

A toothy smile dawned in the midnight of their coal black faces.

"Thank yo, Colonel, thank yo, Sir."

"That goes for me too Sir – double."

"What?"

"Yassa - Lieutenant Jackson he says we good for nuttin cept digging latrines. We been adiggin and adiggin close on five years. But ditches, why - dat's, dat's, dat's, civil engineering - sho – nuf."

To the sophisticated ears of the Colonel it sounded like bitter sardonic irony, but the brothers were sincere enough, digging ditches would make a welcome change of scenery not to mention atmosphere.

"Right, enough of this lollygagging. You are on a charge. What is your name?"

"Watt, Sir."

"I said what is your name?"

"Watt, Sir."

"Are you deaf as well as insolent? What is your name soldier. I am running out of patience."

"Watt, Sir."

"Very well. If that's how you want to play it. The hard way it is then. You can't beat the army, son and you can't beat me. Right Sergeant what is this man's name?"

"Watt, Sir."

"I said - what, oh not you too, what is this a conspiracy? I'll break you so help me. I am in no mood for this Sergeant and if you value those stripes."

"Watt's his name, Sir."

"Yes, whatshisname, but if you can't remember you can't, and this one what is his name?"

"Watt's his name too, Sir."

"Yes whatshisname too, don't try my patience. What is his name?"

"Watt, Sir."

The spectrum of crimson over his brow edged a degree further towards the infrared, and his blood pressure soared another critical milestone. Fearful for his stripes the Sergeant tried to explain.

"You don't understand, Sir. Watts Watt it's as simple as that."

"Don't tell me I don't know what's what you oaf. For in a moment I'm going to give you what for."

Fearful of what the camp grape vine would make of this ridiculous exchange, not to mention the officer's mess or, heaven forbid, it would ever reach the Pentagon, he withdrew his cut-down shot gun with one hand and grabbed Wilberforce's shirt with the other.

"Right, you black son of a bitch. We shall see what's what now," and ripped open Wilberforce's shirt and pulled off his dog tags.

"Watt W. Baptist. Dob 1.4.30" Seconds later he did the same to his brother.

"Watt W. Baptist. Dob 1.4.30"

"Gotcha you commie bastards, forgeries. Both these dog tags are identical. You'll both see the inside of Fort Leavenworth Prison for this."

"Not identical, Sir" interjected the Sergeant. "Numbers are different".

"Yes Sir," added Wilberforce. "Wez brothers, twins in fac, join the army on the very same day we did in Savannah. It was a bright spring day and I sez to Granma ..."

"Shut your goddamn coon mouth you black son of a bitch. I've a good mind to blow your frigging head off."

As if he intended to do just that, he thumbed back both hammers and thrust the gun into Wilberforce's twitching face.

A new stern and authoritative east-coast voice entered the conversation.

"Colonel Peach, what on earth do you think that you are doing treating an enlisted man like that, put that gun away this instant and consider yourself relieved of command."

There, not six feet away and witness to the closing paragraphs of this sad incident, stood General Fishbinder, the inspector general, and his staff.

Red faced one moment, and ashen grey the next, Colonel Peach stunned into mute silence, dropped his trademark gun and both dog tags, turned without a word and loped under a grey cloud of comprehensive despondency to his quarters.

With a pounding head, twitching cheek and trembling hands, he climbed the steps to the veranda of his bungalow like an impoverished bereaved eunuch with toothache. In pain and with nothing to look forward to. The screen door slammed shut behind him.

"You're early dear," said Mary his wife.

"I've just ruined my career," he said voice breaking.

"That's nice dear," she said. She had been drinking since he left the house. With *I Love Lucy*, her favourite show, on television totally attuned to it's canned laughter, she was nicely mellow.

"I'm ruined - it's the end," he said on the verge of tears.

"What dear?" she said from the lounge, trying to shout above the volume of the TV. "What, what was that? What?"

"Oh, Mary not you too, what, what, what."

Emerging from the lounge and steadying herself against the door, she said, "My dear, you do not look well, not at all well, off to bed with you and I will bring you a nice cool glass of my special fruit punch, just you relax. Nothing like fruit punch for heat stroke. It's made with genuine Georgia peach brandy. A little man from your regiment gets it for me. It's delicious and really rather cheap. But land sakes, I do declare it's the best peach brandy in the whole of Dixie." She took a long swallow draining her glass.

"You really must try it, it is so peachy."

# WHEN DREAMS CAME TRUE

C ivil Service clerk Tony Katz took a firm grip on his HMSO ballpoint pen, bent his head as if he were deeply concentrating upon the manilla pocket file before him, closed his eyes and began to day dream. As always he dreamed of being incredibly, fantastically, unbelievably rich. Of living in a hot tropical land far away. A place where clothing would be an unnecessary affectation. A place where he would be surrounded 24/7 by sexually insatiable companions. Ah if only.

This was the way he made the hours of boredom fly by. The work was so simple a child could do it. Put every thing and everyone in their box. Tick, tick, tick box after box, and before you knew where you were it was five o'clock and home time. Today was special, however. It was payday. It was Friday, and Monday was a Bank Holiday.

Deep, deep in his soul he hated this job, and this office. The monotony, the rules and the boredom, but most of all he hated the Indians who worked with him on this side of the benefits counter, and the West Indians who queued up on the other. It made him shudder to think that he might have to do this job for another year, a decade or, heaven forbid, forever.

Still, he told himself, look on the bright side. He had three whole days plus some hours to spend upon his project, his real work; a new microscope and a new kiln to unpack and several novel ideas on new procedures. Tony, like many low grade civil service clerks, had a degree. Sadly a qualification in science was not the key to the prosperous future he had supposed, and like many graduates before him and, no doubt, since had found the civil service to be a convenient place to hide and escape the harsh winds of a recession.

His secret aim was to employ high temperatures, high voltages at high frequencies to convert ordinary carbon dioxide into long flexible strands of almost pure carbon that could be tightly spun into incredibly strong threads and ropes. Stronger than nylon that would never burn, and stronger than steel that would never rust. At the beginning, he had produced a few fibres as thin as spider silk so he knew it could be done. Since then he had failed four thousand, nine hundred and six times. He had his failures and his notes to prove it.

This evening, as he ran up the dingy ill lit stairs to his top floor flat, he told himself as he had told himself so many times before. This was the night. Tonight's results might be the very fulcrum upon which a bright and affluent future depended.

His chest tight with anticipation, he flipped open the door and ran to his bench and the cooling autoclave and … Sadly another failure. What should have been a bunch of incredibly strong carbon filaments was just a misshapen cinder about the size of a cigarette which crumbled into black sand. So, like the methodical scientist which he was, he tipped the residue into a large glass coffee jar, which was now nearly full of failed attempts.

One piece of grit about the size of a pinhead slipped unnoticed through his fingers, and fell into an adjacent Petri dish. Unnoticed that is until he was halfway through an egg and cress sandwich when he became aware of a faint fizzing. Something like an Alka-Seltzer, but not as loud. Now that was odd. The little black cinder was rocking ever so slightly and for a tense moment he was unable to say why. Then he had it. Last week he had cleaned some electrical components in a solution of hydrochloric acid in that very dish. . Putting aside his supper, he dripped a little more acid onto the sample. The reaction was instant. The little cinder crackled and bubbled and skated around the dish upon a skin of acid like a cockroach in torment.

He was not given much to bad language but, "Well I'll be fuff," he muttered as he picked the now quiet sample and washed it in distilled water.

"If I'm not mistaken," he almost squeaked as his throat tightened with excitement. "I have just made a diamond." And why should he not have? A diamond is just carbon, which was subjected long ago to high temperatures in a strong magnetic field in the bowels of the earth where its atoms formed into regular patterns, which became fixed as the earth cooled. Hey presto. A diamond, and by accident in following another dream he had done just the same.

He had just made a diamond and there at the back of his bench stood a coffee jar with about half a kilo of the little darlings. Even if only of industrial quality he had a fortune on his hands. So he went out and got drunk, as any good scientist might. Returning home he climbed the stairs to his rooms, fell once or twice, and burst out laughing at the dusty yellow light that lit the stairwell and landings. "Behold I am Lucifer, the bringer of light to dark places," he said out loud and laughed once again

Fully clothed, he fell on his bed where his dreams came in a familiar flood. The sunshine, the erotic teasing with Mrs Thompson, the landlady, which were based upon nothing at all. Then came the terror dream. He would be bound hand and foot in a small dark space. He screamed but could make no sound louder than the thud, thud, thud, of his heartbeat in his ears. It was the self same nightmare he had had since childhood. A reliving of his life in the womb, his analyst Dr Greenwood had said. Just anxiety. He would grow out of it, but he never did and it was always with profound relief when he awoke to discover it was just another silly childish dream, a pre-natal projection.

Next morning having washed a few more of his cinders in acid, he caught the bus and went to see his Uncle Samuel, a retired jeweller.

"Ah Tony - you come to see your old uncle, first time in so long. Your Aunt Kitty mentioned you only yesterday. Come in and have some coffee, Kitty look who's here."

It had been many years since the old fellow had cut and polished precious stones and these days his hands shook so, but his eye for quality was just as keen as it ever had been.

"Oh yes, hum," he said. "Diamonds," as Tony handed him the small package. "Uncut diamonds, looks OK too. Do you mind?" Mounting a stone in a tool jewellers call a knopf he started up his old polishing table. He no longer traded but he liked to keep his hand in with little jobs. He polished a face of the diamond so that he might look into its heart.

"Good colour, blue white, excellent clarity. Over half a carat I should say." He paused suddenly and turned to Tony, his old grey eyes moist with fear or anger.

"You bloody little fool. Do you know what these are?"

Clearly Tony did but he was not about to talk of a carbon crystal matrix, excited by heat and stabilised by an electromagnetic field on a kitchen table in Camden Town.

"Er, no uncle - so tell me, are they any good?"

"Good, good, they are bloody perfect," his voice suddenly thick with the middle European accent of his youth and supercharged with emotion.

"The only place where stones of this quality come from uncut like this is Zombokki. They are blood stones boy, killing stones. Conflict diamonds. Smuggled out of that cursed country up the arse of some godless schwartzer to buy guns for the communist rebels. Give them back Tony, before you get hurt .... I'm serious son."

Seeing surprise in his nephew's face and misreading it as disbelief he continued.

"You think that your old uncle is a bloody fool, yes? Look at me straight and tell me I am wrong." His stare was level and hard. He was a good judge of men.

"You didn't buy them. Even at bargain basement prices you could never afford them. So you stole them. I don't think so. Therefore you are handling them for somebody else. That somebody else is not a regular dealer, even a crooked one, or he would not need you. So he stole them, but who from? The only people with the nouse and the contacts to turn these stones into guns and tanks are the Russian Mafia. God help us. My advice to you is to put the word out on the street that you are willing to return them ,as er, lost property like for a small fee and trust to your luck You may have to give up your man, but it's survival . I know a lot about survival. I escaped Hitler and survived Stalin. I had to kill four men before I was your age."

From a drawer at the end of a table, with trembling brittle fingers the old man took a worn cardboard box tied up with string which smelled of three in one oil. From it he took a heavy

Walther automatic pistol and the largest flick knife Tony had ever seen, and with a blessing handed them over to Tony saying, "If you can't talk your way out of this you may, God forbid, need these. Don't say a word to your Aunt Kitty about any of this. Quickly put it away. Here she comes with the coffee."

Even though the diamonds were his very own home made variety and no criminals whatsoever were involved, he went along with the charade, pocketed the flick knife and stuck the pistol in his belt. It was exciting to just hold such things and imagine all sorts of romantic scenarios. He set out determined to be the hero of his own life.

A week later he had turned his back on the civil service for good and all. It was like a great oppressive weight had been lifted from his shoulders. Never again would he find himself imprisoned in such a place. He was a man of spirit, and spirits must fly free or die. Still he had to find an outlet for the stones, and really had no idea of where to start. He couldn't just walk into a Hatton Garden dealer with a jolly good day and offer to flog them some diamonds at knock down prices. It was a problem to be sure.

One evening sipping a pint of Young's Special Bitter in *The Flask* public house in Hampstead, he ran into an old school friend, now a police inspector. By degrees over another pint and a curry he turned the conversation around until he found what he needed - the name of a fence.

Now I don't know if you realise this, but doing business with a fence is not like, say off-loading a stolen watch to a laid-back pawnbroker. Your successful fence tends to keep a pretty fair distance between himself and the thief. The first thing you learn, as an apprentice fence, is that thieves are, as a rule, stupid. Invariably they get caught sooner or later, and when they do the first thing they do is offer to throw in a fence to soften their burden. You see, they all feel cheated to only get ten or twenty percent of the haul which lends a certain moral legitimacy to grassing up the fence. Only a mug will see a punter straight in off the street and Claud Vosper was no mug.

Still he was curious when an uncut diamond, followed by another, arrived by post at his Golders Green Office above the best salt beef shop in West London. The card that accompanied each stone simply said, "Want more?" The last card simply said "Hotpoint Iced Diamond for sale. Strimmer accepted in fair exchange. Claud smiled at the play on words. Hot Diamonds, Grass cutter, fair exchange. One could not expect such subtlety from the old bill. By subsequent arrangement, a card was left behind the bar of the *Royal Exchange* pub in Kilburn. It read:

"Ice man please deliver the pitted olives to Rubin's salt beef emporium, Saturday seven o'clock sharp."

Tony walked around the block twice, with his heart in his mouth, a gun in his belt and a huge flick knife, with about £100,000 worth of stones in his pocket. Eventually, he screwed up his courage and climbed the uncarpeted stairs. Claud Vosper was not what he had expected. He wore a kilt for a start. The name was obviously false. Still the   tubby little Indian looked pleased to see him. Perhaps even half-surprised, anticipating some sort of police trick.

Expecting to be treated with suspicion, Tony laid the little fold of paper onto the shabby old-fashioned desk and slowly opened it. The fence pressed a switch and a dusty old crone in a sari shuffled into the room and looked at each stone through a powerful hand held lens, then weighed each and every one on an electronic balance.

The whole added up to five point two five carats. She nodded to Mr Vosper. The fence picked up the fold of paper and said, "Wow , I can see that the fortunes of this young man are about to change most radically. Thank you, Zita, that will be all for now."

The unspoken question which hung into the air was 'How much?'

"Don't look like much do they? And at the end of the day, what are they? Stones, dug out of a hole in the ground for what? A dollar a day, slave wages. Hardly worth a man's life would you say? Hardly worth ten men's lives or for that matter a thousand men's lives. Enough of these, and you can buy a country. Shall we say ten thousand pounds? Would that be fair? All things considered that is."

He had not heard Zita leave the room and did not hear, but half-sensed, a new presence enter. The hairs on the back of his neck bristled, and a chill of fear ran down his spine.

Something flew through the air and landed with a soft thud on the desk. It was a  bundle of fifty pound notes.

"Ten thousand pounds I think you said. I hope that you will spend your reward with discretion Mr. er.. Vosper."

Tony turned to see the largest and most prepossessing African he had ever seen in his life from behind the benefits counter. His dark double breasted blazer with its MCC Badge did nothing to camouflage the 17 stone of hard, uncompromising muscle contained within.

"Allow me to introduce myself, as our host is a little preoccupied with counting at the moment. I am, Chief Inspector M'Bollo of the Zombokki security services. Mr Vosper here has agreed to sell you to me for the princely sum of ten thousand pounds, but I suspect that you are not worth a fraction of that sum. Still a bargain is a bargain. Now, it is incumbent upon your good self to tell me everything about these diamonds - these stolen diamonds. How you came to have them. Who you brought, or stole, them from. In fact you will be kind enough to tell me - everything."

Tony rose to go. "Look here, whoever you are, my business here is with Mr Vosper and I resent being told what to do by a ..."

He did not see the slap coming, but he would remember the stars until his dying day. There followed a violent cuffing, which went on for about a fortnight, or so it seemed. At some point he must have made the decision to tell the truth, and would have told all, but at the moment the words, "I made them" passed his split lips the Walther pistol fell out of his belt and clattered upon the bare floor. Why hadn't he thought of it before? He could have shot his way clear. Too late now, but there was still the flick knife, but the instant he drew it a blow from Mr M'Bollo's huge fist dismissed all other considerations from his mind, and he collapsed upon the floor.

It was not until the *M V Goldfinch* was south west of Gibraltar that he was released from his little dark crate and given a drink of water, taken to the captain's cabin and slapped some more. Pieces were slowly and systematically carved from his toes. So he talked and talked. In fact he wouldn't stop talking, but he strongly suspected that his interrogator knew nothing of electro chemistry, nothing of phased flux density or the various isotopes of carbon. It was in vain that he told them, and then told them again, that he had made the bloody things. Didn't they speak English? Evidently they did not.

Upon arrival at Port Quangi he tried again, and again at his trial which was equally futile. Not only were the diamonds against him, but the gun and the flick knife did nothing to convince the court of his good character. The white-wigged judge, in a fair impersonation of a half of Guinness, told him that he was an imperialist and a very bad man who ought to be shot, but he, having been called to the bar in Lincoln's Inn was inclined to leniency and sentenced him to ten years hard labour. Tony was dragged from the court in tears, bundled into a Land rover and taken to Zimbokki's Number three Pipe as the diamond mine was called.

There he was to shovel the blue clay half a mile underground in temperatures which never varied more than half a degree. Here at the deepest level only the worst criminals worked in the stifling damp heat and dim half light.

Back in London it is safe to say that women did not find him attractive in the least. Here in Africa in his dark, steamy, underground prison his fellow inmates found this thin, pale, naked, young white man to be a most endearing companion, not to say arousing. His resistance to the first rape cost him his front teeth and the sight in one eye, the second merely a broken nose, at which point he completely lost the will to live and sought release in the half-conscious twilight world of recollections, dreams and fantasies never far from a blissful oblivion. Here his nights were as tormented as his days, time marked only by the starting and stopping of the donkey engine, which worked the small elevator which carried the spoil to the surface. It started up on the hour of seven and its knock, knock, knock, diesel echoed swiftly along the tunnels and dark chambers sounding like a heartbeat, bringing back into Tony's dreams, memories of his childhood nightmares as explained away in a sunlit Harley Street consulting room by his analyst Dr Greenwood, as deep and distant womb memories.

Reassured that it was all a horrible dream he fell into a deep sleep from which, mercifully he never awoke.

# EPILOGUE

The epilogue to this tale you might care to compose for yourself, but I might suggest an appropriate start.

Following his sudden disappearance, his room was cleared of his possessions and what couldn't be sold to offset his arrears of rent found their way into an Essex landfill site where, many years later, coastal erosion uncovered and caused a coffee jar to rock uneasily back and forth in the dark tidal silt until a sharp-eyed beach comber, such as yourself, picked it up and …

Oh, you tell me how it ends. It is after all just a dream.

# BAA BAA BLACK SHEEP

I t was a small dusty village way out in the bush; a cluster of neglected timber houses, and a tin-spired church, red with rust, which cast a lengthening shadow along the dry main street in a gratuitous gift of direction elsewhere. Opposite the church, a crude hand-painted sign of a red dragon proclaimed in defiance of the elements 'cool beer - last chance for 50 miles' and underneath in small letters 'iron-monger and grocer.' Just enough to keep body and soul together. Not much of a town perhaps but a regular oasis to a footsore traveller whose old Morris van had died the death ten miles or so back along a dirt road heading in the general direction of Black Stump on the way to nowhere.

I must have looked a right old sight even by the limited sartorial standards of those parts as I stumbled in to the pub, my tongue a cinder in my mouth. 'Strewth, a pom refugee. Just about done in too. Quick Barney give this pilgrim a beer before he spontaneously combusts. I can feel the heat from here,' said a stocky, powerfully built man at the bar. As a rule I don't care for lager beer, but this one tasted like the amber nectar of the advertisements. So good in fact, that I stood a round for my good Samaritan and his pals at the bar, even though it ate up the last of my cash. Still, I had a feeling that my luck was about to change, and it did too.

With re-hydrated vocal chords I asked 'how did you know I was English? Is it that obvious under all this dust?'

'No mate' said my benefactor. 'Constable Evans from Barry, the last town you passed through, told us over the radio that someone was on his way in a beat up van that didn't sound at all healthy. If you hadn't got here before sunset, one of the boys here would have gone for a look see. You can't get lost round here mate, we've got eyes and ears everywhere. No place to get lost and, if you're up to no good, no place to hide. You're safer here than you would be in the Old Kent Road - me old cock sparrow.' He added in a passable cockney accent no doubt to make me feel right at home. How was he to know that I was from Cheltenham?

'That's truer than you realise,' I said extending my hand 'Jack. Jack Thorougood, the world's worst opal miner. In eighteen months I have found just enough quality stones to keep me in beer, boots, and diesel for my old van.'

'Pete,' he replied. 'Pete Williams. That's Barney behind the bar and these two sinners are

Boomer and Dingo.' Barney had the round fleshy face of a baby raised on vinegar and Brussel sprouts who had not been burped for 40 years, whilst Boomer and Dingo looked ready to audition for the part of Abel Magwich. 'Utterly worthless the three of them,' he said as only a close friend can say.

'Mind you Jack, they might not look like angels, but they do a lot of work for our little church here.' Boomer and Dingo raised their near empty glasses, grinning like a couple of U-boat Captains on bonus sailing off with a full set of torpedoes on board.

Pete's voice dropped to a deeper and more serious tone.

'Tell me mate, er Jack. Is it true what we hear on the radio about all the problems you're having back home; the riots and all? The total breakdown of law and order in some places. Armed gangs, war lords and stuff. Can that be right? It beggars belief.'

'Well you better believe it, Pete, and it's not problems it's problem - singular.'

The pub, already quiet, fell silent. Outside in the gathering darkness an animal howled, whether in ecstasy or pain I couldn't say. Taking a sip of beer I said at length, 'Welshman. Pure and simple. Bloody Welshmen. There is not a creature on God's earth as cruel and evil as these bloody Welsh'.

He raised his eyebrows as Boomer and Dingo looked to him to respond and Barney trapped a red backed spider that had wandered across the bar under a beer glass. I shuddered and just for the briefest of moments felt a curious empathy for this sad creature, bewildered and trapped in a strange environment. 'Just hold on there mate, that's a bit harsh isn't it? I know quite a few Welshmen, good as gold. I won't hear a word said against the Welshies.'

Which was not the response I expected.

'Well, yes, speak as you find, Pete. Good and bad in all sorts I suppose. Come to think of it I've met a couple of bloody fine Welshmen.'

Why I said that I don't know, cowardice I suppose.

'There's er, um, ah - Harry Secombe. Lovely voice Harry and er, um, of course, Dylan Thomas. Not that I ever met him of course. "Do not go softly into that good night" - Dylan Thomas.'

'God Bless him,' they all mouthed silently, which I found damned odd at the time.

'You see Pete, it's these bloody fundamentalists that are at the heart of the problem. Stirring up the unemployed riff raff, the pig ignorant and the easily led.'

Pete and Barney, and Boomer and Dingo exchanged knowing glances and for a moment it felt like someone had just walked over my grave.

'It's not just me airing my prejudices Pete, even the Bishop of Hartford has said as much. What did he say, oh yes, he said "Their God can't be much of a God if he has to get an ignorant rabble to do his bidding. A real true God could strike down anyone at any time. Or touch their hearts for that matter. A real honest to goodness God didn't need a lynch mob to mete out his justice."

'Well that got him into deep trouble. Not only were the fundamentalists after his hide but the government, our own bloody government, had him arrested for inciting racial hatred. How about that? Cos I blame the government all along. Bloody Labour Government giving them their own parliament. Mind you, who could have disagreed with that at the time? People have a right to self-determination and all that. But it didn't stop there. They started to make their own laws. Gently at first. Regulating the school's curriculum, Sunday opening hours, and stuff like that. They lifted VAT on woollen goods. In fact I financed this venture by smuggling duty-free socks into England. Ultimately they insisted in establishing holy Druidic law and not a whisper of protest from Westminster.

'After all diversity and multi-culturalism was the order of the day. Anyone who did raise a voice in objection was branded a fascist or racist and cowed into silence, often by the police. Political correctness gone completely bloody mad. They opened their own churches, well chapels, all over the place and woe betide you if you didn't stop what you were doing when the call to prayer went out. In Welsh, of course, everything had to be in Welsh although not that more than a few of the faithful could understand above half a dozen words."

Once I'd started I had to get all the pent-up anger, which had turned me into an exile off of my chest. My audience sat enthralled. 'Red hot stuff it is too. Fire and brimstone pouring down upon the heads of apostates, back sliders and unbelievers. That's us right? Real mean, heavy frightening stuff. Well, their followers believe it, or say they do. It's all so much mumbo jumbo. Praying five times a day whilst a Druid goes on and on about green valleys for the good and hell's fire for the disobedient. You should see them trembling and shaking at – quote - "the Word." God help them if they don't do it. Here, Barney, let me have another beer on tick will you?'

He served it promptly and I took a long pull.

'And then there's their women folk all togged out in black hats and all, right out of the 17th Century. No choice either. Quite pretty too, some of them, in an elfish sort of way. Always carrying something they are, harp, spinning wheel, sack of coal. You mustn't laugh or say a word about it. Get this. The women will tell you that it's an expression of their freedom to be Welsh. Which is pathetic if you like. Freedom to conform, to do as you're told. What sort of freedom is that?

'But what really frightens me are the sons of Glendower and the barmy army Yakki-Dar Freedom Fighters up in the hills. Suicide bombers with their Kalishnikov AK47s and RPGs.

The kids are all brainwashed as well. You should see them try to disco dance to Men of Harlech and stuff like that. It's got so that they won't eat their dinner unless the lamb or whatever it is has been put to death by a Druid with a magic knife who has to say the magic words to make it fit to eat. Do you know that you can't open a butchers or a grocers now unless you have a Druid on the payroll? And, I ask you, who appoints the Druids? Why other Druids of course that's who. What a con.

It's a licence to print money. A Druid can order a woman to be stoned to death with lumps of coal for having a bit on the side. A man can get 50 lashes if he fills out an official form in blue ink, or puts down anything except chapel in the box marked religion.

'Touchy too, like you wouldn't believe. The least protest or suggestion that it is all a monstrous scam, and the Druids will call a mob out on to the streets.'

I took a sip of beer.

'We have a comedian at home called Jim Dunaldson who made a rather silly joke about a lonely hill farmer and a little sheep called Bronwin on his TV show. Next thing you know there was a bounty of a million pounds to the man that killed him and esponged the insult. Television sets were piled up on street corners and burnt. Broadcasting House in London was besieged by a howling mob and pelted with transistor radios. Copies of the *Radio Times* were burnt in Parliament Square. The Prime Minister called for calm and claimed that his father knew Lloyd George. And why does the government put up with it? Because the buggers are sitting on all the coal. Just like OPEC only worse.

'I can't say if it was wilful provocation, insensitivity or ignorance but the very next night after the Jim Dunaldson show, they just had to run the film *Shaun the Sheep* on Channel 4, on a Sunday too. Next day Hamley's Toy Shop in Regent Street was smashed up by 100,000 enraged Welshmen, and a million pounds worth of fluffy sheep were ripped limb from limb and burnt under their blasphemy laws. Armed gangs roamed the streets in droves looking for anyone not wearing wool. It all went a bit quiet during the Pilgrimage season when all true believers have to go on something called the Eisteddfod. Get their Welsh passports stamped and become entitled to use the honourific 'Taffy' before their name. It was about then that I decided to take my acrylic sweater and get out for good, as far away from those insane fanatical fundamentalist bastards as I could, before they got their hands on an atomic bomb. God help the free world then, I hope that I never see another bloody sheep for as long as I live.'

Visibly controlling his disquiet, or his temper, Pete brought my story to an abrupt end with, 'Sorry to hear that mate because just down the road apiece on the other side of the Bulonga-Wonga river there are a couple of million of the little darlings. Be this way too after the rains when the grass picks up a bit. Me, I just love em.'

Just then as I drained the very last drop of the amber nectar I heard the most awful unsettling sing-song sound via a tinny and crackling loud speaker out in the street.

48

'What on earth is that Pete?' I asked. 'It sounds like an abbo having his bulla bong bitten off by a wombat. Sounds sort of Welsh too.'

'Yes, boyo. It's the call to prayer,' he said as he and the boys stood and made for the door. Turning he added by way of a parthian shot 'Must be off Jacko, we'll have to continue this very interesting conversation when we get back, won't we boys? After all you're not going anywhere are you?'

Which was true. I wasn't.

# SOME DAY SOON

M e. What do I do? Now there's a question. Yes. That's a question alright, but as you ain't from around these parts I'll tell you. If in you will fill my glass that is."

"Ta, oh, that's better, you're a gent. Ooops musn't say that, not no more. That's one of the forbidden words that is. When I was a boy there was lots of gents and ladies too. In them days there was lots of ladies and gentlemen in nice big black cars with big houses and gardens an such. Loverly. Mind you we also had lots of skin heads, punks, goths, queers, chavvies and more nig-nogs in more different shades of black an brown than you could shake a stick at. All gone now of course along with the words to call em. Still times change. Here's health.

"Oh yeah, what do I do? Well I'm the bloke what has to collect the Stiggies and Stapps.

"What are they? Coo, mate, where you been living for the last fifty years, on the moon?

"Oh I'm sorry. Well, well, well, you don't look the sort.

"Never heard of Stiggies and Stapps. Well see this, this silver band around me throat. Well that is a Stapp. And this little square thing I has here in my pocket. That's a Stiggie.

"Babies have them fitted in their tiny nut. Only certain sorts of baby mind . Nice uns from nice clean homes. Then as they grow up they sort of know stuff without ever learning it. So when one of the governors wants a new bridge or an airport he presses a few buttons on a big white cabinet up there in London someplace, an a whole bunch of people stops whatever they are a doing of and goes off and builds a bridge. Just like that, clever aint it?

"Thirsty work this jawing. That's very kind of you, same again, but ask Arry to slosh a bit of gin in it. That's what we call a dog's nose that is. That is, did call it. Back in the day when there was dogs, and cats and rats and mice. All done away with now of course - unhealthy see.

"Ah , thank you. Good drop of gulpers that is. I could stay here all day talking to you. You being such a good conversationalist that is. I'm learning a lot talking to you so I am.

"Now, where were we, oh yes the others. Kids from mean dirty homes like mine. Homes where the old man is a fighter, a red protester say, or an agitator. The sort to smash up computers and stuff like that. Coo he couldn't half use his fists, my old man. See here, he knocked that tooth clear out of my head on my 18th birthday. No special reason. Just so I knew what's what and didn't think that I was old enough to give him any old lip. God bless him. Made me the man I am today.

"Now us , we were the sort that couldn't be trusted to be policemen or build bridges and things in case we became rebellious, tried to change the system an all that, so we get the Stapps. One wrong action, word or deed and a Stiggie can throttle you simply by thinking about it. It's horrible, everything starts to go black and you can't breath and you fall over. Don't know exactly how that works because its solid metal and it don't move at all but it chokes you just the same.

"First of all there were ructions; nobody wanted to have them fitted. One riot after another. So the cunning buggers backed off and waited until you had been arrested for something. Any bloody thing at all. In my case I filled out a driving licence form in blue ink instead of black. I got seven days inside and this. For some people it was a mark of status to start with like they was a big gangster or something. But when you are on your knees in the gutter with some big Stiggie cop grinning down at you, you think different. Well my friend you learn pretty quick not to answer back, not look insolent, not meet in secret with restless and rebellious company, as the saying goes. The last time it happened to me, my third time I think, I nearly died. Some people never learn and in the end they do die. Gentlemen of an independent frame of mind at one end and the multicultural sweepings of the world's gutters at the other end.

"Now sunny Jim, if you was as old as me you would see the difference. Nowadays there are avenues of trees where there used to be huge traffic jams. Parks full of flowers instead of council estates full of litter and used hypodermic needles. It's alright now I suppose, someone has to keep order after all is said an done.

"There are some folk though who really want to go back to the olden times. All that noise, danger and dirt. The endless worry. The quest for freedom they calls it. Silly beggars. Ha.

"Freedom to riot, freedom to get mugged. Freedom to go out and nick stuff. Freedom to have more kids than you can afford. Freedom to live on the 23rd floor of a concrete block of flats with neighbours who feel free to piss in the lifts, and shoot up on the stairs. Now I don't say that it was like that everywhere but for some of us it was an everyday reality.

"Still there's no going back, not now things is nice and settled like. Mind you there are some silly kids, mostly from nice soft homes who work themselves up into a right old state, day after day until they cant take it any more and jump under a train or off a roof. Dozens of em some days. Though today's is a bit quieter than usual . When they do, it's my job to go along and pick up the Stiggie, occasionally a Stapp. Wash off the blood and stuff . Take it back to the depot, get a receipt . Bloody hot on procedures they are. Then some other bloke will take it to bits and see why it went wrong before it gets put back into the system like. A good job that, eight hour day, nice warm workshop, coffee machine, free lunch . But you have to be a Stiggie yourself to get a job like that.

"They would never give a job like that to a Stappie. Not in a thousand years."

# THE NEXT TIME AROUND

A secret, a real secret, a secret worthy of silence creates a bond between its conspirators. An unspoken secret doubly so. Lips may be sealed with stitches of fear, doubt, shame, guilt, love, reticence, sadness or duty. No contractual small print could ever produce a more air tight covenant.

That Doctor Charles shared such a secret was evident in his soft brown eyes; eyes which had ever only lied with difficulty. That much about himself he knew. Both he and his patient knew that the end was near, but neither said a word to the other. It was their secret.

He was about to light another cigarette and pour another coffee when the telephone in the hall rang. Its old fashioned bell harsh and insistent. He was half expecting a call at this hour, breakfast time. It was always breakfast time. He sighed heavily as his wife called up the stairs, "Charles, it's Alice."

With the greatest effort and no small discomfort Victor Henstridge rolled to the side of the bed and began to retch over the chipped white enamel basin there. Nothing came of course. He had lived on an intravenous glucose drip for weeks, still he felt easier just the same. Had he made the slightest sound in his exertions, nurse McKinnon -making herself a cup of tea in the next room - would have been in like a shot. In spite of her tiredness she was alert to every little sound, and the old house at this time of night, just before dawn, was alive with odd thumps, creaks and groans but her ears were attuned to the sounds of her patient.

He lay back on the huge pillow, his mind investing the wind in the chimney with anguished howls, lamentations, sobs and melancholic moans.

There was a little blood in his mouth but he felt strangely at peace notwithstanding his exhaustion as if, and he could frame the thought no better, as if he had passed an important milestone. In part it was because the pounding in his head had ceased and his breathing, although slow and laboured, had settled into a resigned and stoic pace.

But yes, there was something else too, and for a moment he couldn't pin it down; determine what it was. Something had changed. Something was truly different. All this I might add transpired in no more than a second or two. The pain had gone, really gone, as it did from time to time, but apart from that, what was it?

Yes, yes, he had it now, yes.

This was what it was like to feel normal; well again. Although as he surely knew, he had a mind which was all too easily deceived, but even so - delusion or not - whilst it lasted he would enjoy it. Suck every ounce of comfort from the reprieve until its pith and peel turned insipid on the tongue, and bitter tears welled up in his eyes, for everything tender and good which might have been a salvation in his shallow pointless wasted little life. Tears for what might have been, and truly could have been if only he had managed things differently at each of life's little junctions.

Somehow though, this feeling, strange and welcome as it was, was different from the ease induced by the Diamorphine cocktail he had become accustomed to. It was more subtle, loaded with nuances, kinder and less instantly gratifying.

It was more like, how shall I put this, for it is never easy to put a paradox into an exact perspective; it was, in some strange way - which neither he nor I could explain - kindred to the first violent stab of anguish he had experienced when he had been shocked out of his denial and forced to accept that his illness was real and terminal.

Euphoria now bore him upon a cushion of hovercraft expectation as wonderful and fleeting as a burst of spring sunshine upon a carpet of bluebells. And there, just for a split second, he even managed to picture nurse McKinnon without her clothes, hair down and lips slightly parted. I must be on the mend he thought for a lovely moment before reality censored both thought and fantasy and the warm, pink, round image sank into a morass of doubt and quickly faded, leaving scant imprint upon his consciousness. Ah, still it was lovely whilst it lasted.

A gap in the curtains foretold an imminent rosy dawn and the assurance that within half an hour the sun would be up over the ridge behind Eastlea Farm, and its warm vanguard would be inching its way down the estuary valley, opening the flowers in its path and guzzling up the haze.

Now that was odd, just there, did you catch that? No of course not, but he did. Even from behind closed windows the smell of the sea was overpowering. He smelt it as he had never smelt it before. No, that's a lie. He smelt it as he had not smelt it since he was a child on what was perhaps his first visit to the seaside. Folkestone that would have been then. Lemonade or Tizer and crisps with a little blue bag of salt. Winkles that you had to capture with a pin, and pink candyfloss which somehow attracted all the grime in Kent to the stickiness around a small boys mouth.

BOOM
That was the coastguard. They were going to launch the lifeboat; the new orange one. This he had to see.

He swung his thin brown legs to the floor, remembering that he hadn't stood upright for a month. He expected to feel dizzy but no, he felt fine. Still a little nauseous perhaps, but not dizzy . In fact he felt very much his own man. The sun was more than half way up now and it shone squarely in his face. Ah, ah, good morning old friend he said in mock greeting, Long time no see . Still he held on to the heavy drapes for the illusion of support they provided.

Yes, yes, there they go. Billy Monk skidding his motorcycle to a halt beside the Lifeboat Station, and Jack Herring tearing down the hill on his sister June's pink bicycle. He was off it before it stopped and he left it, wheels spinning as it lay in the gravel. June would have his guts for garters so she will. Especially after last time. There is the new bloke, Phil something, parking his car.

Hark at those gulls. They know something is up. A lost soul will be joining their number before the day is out, you mark my words.

Come along slowcoach. Albert Roswell, nearest the station and last to arrive, as usual.

Under the urging of strong hydraulic arms the great doors clattered back and the boat began to move down the slipway, its screws turning in hungry anticipation of their first bite of the ocean . A muffled whomp, and a blossom of white foam as the broad bows cut the water heading for the open sea.

"I am so glad," he said out loud, or so he thought, "To have seen another launch, the new boat too. See the boys hop to it for the last time."

The Last Time.

The words hung on his Vaseline-smeared lips and echoed around inside his head in no great hurry to gently fade. One last time they whispered as somewhere close a glass tumbler crashed to the floor and the bedroom door flew open.

Nurse McKinnon paused as she entered the room, her plump and pleasant round features frozen and her mouth a little open in a soft sigh. Tenderly she picked up the thin brown arm which hung over the side of the bed feeling for a pulse, which was no longer there.

"Oh my. What's become of you Victor boy," he found himself saying to the gaunt wretched sad parody of himself laying lifeless in his bed.

With an affection approaching reverence Nurse Alice McKinnon, having found no pulse, shone a little torch into his eyes . First this one then the other, before gently folding his arms across his chest, and closing his eyes with practiced familiarity before finally drawing a sheet up over his face.

He imagined that she intoned a little prayer beneath her breath as she left the room and quietly closed the door, but in truth she was just remembering the telephone number of Doctor

Charles in the village.

"Thank you nurse. Thank you for everything. I don't suppose that I was an easy patient." He paused to get his bearings, hardly glancing at the body on the bed. "Well, that's that. Goodbye Victor. Dying was not so bad after all. The children, the grandchildren will take it hard. Especially Henry, big sentimental lump. He's sure to blub. God bless him. He loved his granddad."

But, hold on, what's this? Unseen hands were clutching at him. Cold resolute hands.

"No, no, not yet. Get off, there's no hurry. Please not yet, a little longer. I'm not ready".

Ready or not he felt like ice as he struggled against their insistent pull, but it was futile and in vain. He was being drawn towards the window and the dawn. "Look, hold on, sod off." but it was no use. As if all the pain and uncertainty of the last few months wasn't enough, he was to be bullied now and dragged about. He had never been so afraid in the whole of his long life. The more he struggled the harder they pulled.

Out of the house and into the sunlight, for it was now full daylight. How easily they had passed through the fabric of the window. Matter is mostly empty space as any science student will tell you.

Up, up into the crisp air, round and round. Caused by fear or motion I cannot say, but he felt sick once again.

The village on the far side of the river began to shimmer, unnaturally so, if I am any judge.

Look, Masons Bakery, the white building just to the left of the church see it, there. One moment the roof was red next it was grey. The tiles had given way to slate. How odd. The mean little speculative houses on the edge of the village were disappearing too. Good riddance. The municipal car park was green again. Elm trees were popping up fully grown and in leaf up on the ridge overlooking the village. Will you look there. Look at that. The hedgerow which had once separated East Field from Home Farm was back as if it had never been ripped out.

The swinging sign outside the *Saucy Sailor* had reverted to its old name *The Coach and Horses* and in front a Triumph Mayflower, a Ford Popular and a Humber Super Snipe, parked next to a Panther Motorcycle and sidecar combination.

"Uncle George had one just like that when I was a boy," he said. "It was hand painted blue just like that and I could swear it was the same one with that little pennant flying from the mudguard which said Torquay."

Before he had given himself time to choose his words he said, "I do believe I am going back in time. Like a drowning sailor I suppose, reviewing my past life."

It might have been a good time for a philosopher to reflect upon the nature of time and life and death and destiny, but he was no philosopher and as easily distracted under the circumstances as you would be yourself.

"Just look at that. The old prefab school and the big boys all in their cricket whites. Why that big fat bugger is Barry Martin, dumb ox, swinging his bat around like a club. Why he caught me a proper whack on the head doing just that, bloody fool. I had to have an x-ray over at the county hospital. Concussion the Doctor said, but I never got any time off school though."

He was about to say something about Miss Green the Headmistress with her austere haircut, her thick ankles, and brown stockings which barely reached her fat knees, when right on cue there she was on the school steps swinging the brass hand bell, which marked the end of playtime for the younger children.

The sound of the bell rose up in the cool morning air to greet his still-spinning body, revolving slowly as he sought to find a centre of gravity, but failing miserably. Everything was shimmering again and the bell was getting louder. Ker-lang, ker-lang, ker-lang. The sound hurt but only on one side of his head. Stranger still he had stopped floating and stopped spinning, and in an instant turned from a dithering balloon to a determined stone. Down, down, down he plunged towards the sound of the bell. Rushing wind filled his ears as the ground rose up to meet him. Closer, ever closer. He could smell the grass now. Then darkness. Then silence. The silence of the grave, or so he thought. Darkness so solid and profound that he could reach out and touch it, but he had no sensation in his hands. He struggled to think, but no thoughts could penetrate the thick inky darkness. Only feelings remained, like sacred whispers in church. His feelings, which were calm and reassuring one minute and fearful to the point of terror the next, and by degrees this dichotomy increased as the first maggots of thought wormed their inquisitive way through whatever remained of his being. Now he could smell incense, sweet and not at all unpleasant, and if he were to hazard a guess he would have said pipe tobacco.

"OK old son, just lie there, don't try to sit up. Miss Green has sent for your mum. You're OK. That clot Barry Martin has just biffed you on the nut with a cricket bat. Not deliberately, just a silly accident that's all. Still it's six of the best for young Mr Martin at assembly tomorrow morning. I expect that you'd like to see that now wouldn't you? I know I would in your place. Just lie quiet, here comes your mum."

With his mother on one side, and Mr Grimwold, the English master, on the other he was eased gingerly into Mr Hurd's taxi and carted off to hospital for his x-ray.

All memories of Nurse McKinnon, morphine, bed sores, glucose drips and terminal cancer were completely forgotten.

Forgotten, that is until the next time around.

# SHOOTING STAR

I t was not a fast ship. Quite unremarkable really and by the standards of its time and place, small and underpowered for its type. But it was there when he needed it and it was so very, very easy to steal.

The war and the economic confusion which invariably followed had given him a fair head start and with each mile his confidence increased, but they were after him now and to some purpose. How was he to have known that hidden deep within the ship's computers were highly classified files, the contents of which, if made public, would bring down the government and fan the embers of a new conflict? The authorities were all too aware of the danger, and were after him now with all the forces at their disposal.

The military had far larger vessels than this with devastating weaponry, not that the civil police were unarmed. Their brand new Point Five cruisers could travel at half the speed of light.

I must explain that all long distance craft in those days employed hydrogen as a fuel. The military had its bunkering stations of course, and the police cruisers could scoop up the four or five atoms of hydrogen present in each square metre of empty space. Not much you might say, but when the mouth of the scoop is the size of a house and travelling at half the speed of light, an enormous quantity may be captured to flow through the core of a nuclear engine to blast the vessel forward at the leading edge of a wave of hot ionised plasma.

The fugitive was not so fortunate, as the ship which he had stolen was a bulk carrier and he needed water. Water which could be split into oxygen for his life support systems, and hydrogen for his hungry engines, without which they would not run and would rapidly overheat to the point of destruction, forming a small black hole in the process. It was a difficult choice. To spend time searching for water or run as far and as fast as he could before his tanks ran dry and he had to escape in a lifeboat and chance that he would not be destroyed in the fall out from eruption when the motors finally went up.

The one bright piece of good fortune in this dark exercise was that he had found two watery planets in the same solar system, one mostly blue and green, the other red. He chose the red one. It was easier on his optics.

It takes a long time, many decades in fact, to strip a planet of its oceans, but he had time, or so he believed, for was he not immortal? Excluding accidents, he might live forever. It was an immortality with little prospect of ever achieving the evolution he so earnestly desired if the authorities ever caught up with him.

Space was infinite and the area which they had to search increased with the cube of the distance from home. A tremendous area even with their huge resources and their desperate need to bring matters to a safe conclusion and avert another war.

On the other hand they were relentless and would not be still until their charged particle weapons had ripped him from stem to stern and his nuclear core had exploded. Not that they would hang about after a confirmed hit. The blast danger would be too great. How badly they wanted him back is evidenced by the search being one of only nine all vessel alerts in all time.

At this point in the narrative I ought to explain something of the make up of the fugitive although in no way an apologist for his behaviour. I will not sanction treason, rebellion, bad faith and grand theft.

He was a single organism, and the best visual description I can give you is to ask that you remember your first lessons in biology when you looked through a microscope for the first time at an amoeba, and saw how it reproduced by splitting into two new creatures, neither being the parent of the other. To all intents and purposes immortal. He could split off at will fully conscious independent creatures who all knew what he knew; were him, in fact, but separate. So a part of him could be on constant watch for pursuit, while another supervised the loading of the precious water, millions and millions of gallons of it, in the huge hold. Weightless in the zero gravity of space, another individual could service the highly radioactive motors, even though death of that self-same individual was a certainty after a short while.

In a moment of idle curiosity he sent a small probe to see with his own eyes, albeit at one remove, what conditions were like on the other planet, the blue one which was apparently devoid of life. Even in a small, fast, craft it took time to travel from the red to the blue planet; time he did not really have, not now for, although his tanks were almost full and the planet bled dry, except for a rime of ice at poles, the police had arrived upon the scene. As he prepared to leave the police commander gave the order to open fire. They should have waited for even at the speed of light it takes precious time to reach a target at long range, time enough for him to abandon the conduit and get under way.

First he had to swing around the planet, then the sun, using its tremendous gravity to hurl him onward into deep space where he would need all his skill and cunning to evade destruction or capture. On his second pass around the planet he engaged his main motor and broke away sunward. The G Forces were unbelievable but being of a gelatinous morphology, he merely flattened out over the whole interior surfaces of the craft until he was a millimetre thick. Not a comfortable expression of his being but endurable. The water in the hold lost its fluidity and he walls bulged. The engines fluttered into life. The Martian water, rich in salts, iron and alkaline metals, obviously agreed with the mechanism and the speed rapidly mounted.

He whipped past the sun on a fine tangent and although still under the pull of its gravity, sped away. Soon, soon now he would be free. Free. As free as a ----------------It was at that precise moment that he realised that in all the excitement he had forgotten to recall the probe sent to the blue and green planet. He tried to contact it, for it was his. It was him, but like a man who has lost a limb, he felt its existence still, but contact was impossible. He must write it off. The speed, the solar wind, the earth's magnetosphere had cut him off for ever. He wondered if that little part of him would seed and flourish, and perhaps in a million years or so he would return to see if it had evolved as he himself would wish to evolve. He did not wonder for long. Not then he didn't. The time for speculation would come later. For the police were now at a range where they could not miss with magazines charged and the firing circuits uncomfortably hot in anticipation of an immanent violent discharge.

Their searching fingers of charged, high energy particles found him out searing through bulkheads and pipelines cutting off the supply of hydrogen to his nuclear converter, causing it to rapidly overheat. The automatic over-ride ejected the critical core within seconds and sent it spinning headlong towards the surface of the sun. With far more significant display the tanks ruptured. The water under pressure sprayed out into space where it instantly turned to ice in the intense cold. Not wishing to remain in the vicinity of a nuclear core which might explode at any moment the police withdrew to return to other duties.

Justice had been done.

Viewing his change of circumstances with considerable stoic calm, he realised that he was in for a long, a very long hibernation. If he kept still he would have enough latent energy to last a million years; two million with any luck. A small part of him had splashed down, safely he hoped, in the warm ocean of a new world.

He liked to comfort himself with the thought that some millennia in the future his descendents would look to the night sky, their hearts drawn to a home they had never known. He was sure that by degrees they would find ways to reach outwards to the stars. It was a scenario he would re-run many times over. He could wait, for he had no option but to wait. He still waits.

Was there something in his genetic make up which would predispose his descendents to theft, treason, rebellion and bad faith? All things that had been a part of his life for so long. We shall just have to wait and see how these earth people turn out. Perhaps somewhere, someday, someone with a little more imagination than average would look up at the red planet that had once had oceans much like their own and wonder where all that water had gone. Perhaps that self-same watcher of the skies looking at the regular reappearance of a comet made mostly of ice on its long seventy-year orbit might put two and two together and the beginning of the end of a long, long prison sentence may at last be in sight.

# THY WILL BE DONE

W ell, that about wraps it up boys," said Bill McGraw, tossing aside a big wrench which raised a small cloud of dust as it landed upon the parched earth. "Let us draw our pay, and get the hell out of this God-damn country." With a screwdriver lifted from the belt of one of his roughnecks, he unscrewed a brass plate from the complex arrangement of valves known to all oilmen as a Christmas Tree. It read: BP Exploration Well KW 8876. Production Well PP 44391 (Z). He was, he felt sure, entitled to a little memento.

"Do you know, Harry", he said returning the screwdriver. "Do you know I was here back in the day when this gusher came in? Came in good too and we sucked her dry, didn't we just. Dryer than a cockroach in a taco oven. Jesus Christ, and here I am in at the death. It's kinda spooky. The last producing oil well, in the last producing field in the whole of Arabia. What we going to do now boss?" It was an honest question from an oilman in a world about to run out of oil.

"I don't know about you boys, but I got a couple of hundred acres up in the Oregon woods and a little 30-foot fishing boat tied up alongside Hendersons Quay there. Why, I'm going to retire buddy, catch enough fish to keep me in groceries, and rip up some lumber for extras. And I reckon that will just about see me out."

"No boss, I mean the world. What's the world going to do without oil?"

"Oh the world will make out I guess. It always has. Go back to horse and buggies. There you go Al, get in ahead of the game. Al Pressburger's…..the best buggie whips money can buy."

The others laughed as the Arab boy with the Coca Cola concession came up pushing his red and white ice box on wheels.

Bill McGraw took a can and gave the boy a twenty dollar note.

"Sorry chief, no change."

"Now don't you worry none about that son. I think that you're going to need it. The oil is all gone and we're going home."

"Ah", said the boy, raising his palms to heaven as if expecting them to be filled. "Insha Allah. It is the will of God. Insha Allah. God bids me return to my flocks and walk the paths our fathers walked."

"You hear that boys? It's God's will. So let's climb into that truck and head west before he strikes you sinners down, because if I know what's on your mind just now you can bet he sure does."

And with that they departed laughing, and the desert knew them no more.

*****

Not too many years later, far to the north in a windswept and grey Edinburgh, Andrew Sykes and Dean Pickavant sank another pint of bitter and said for the thousandth time, "We done it. We bloody well done it. We, the wee boys done it."

"Well as long as you dis'ne do it in here I dinna care," said Angus the barman at the *Waverley Arms.*

"Well we might just do that my wee man and serve you right if we did, so it will."

They had been drinking since lunchtime and after a long period of poverty-enforced abstinence and protracted study, they were entitled to let off steam and be a bit silly. They were students after all was said and done, and within a year their names would be household words.

"Well, what is it yous two has done?"

"Come here," said Dean. "I must whisper".

"Yes shush," said Andrew as they drew their heads together like Popish conspirators.

"We," began Dean. "Yes we, him and me, or should that be he and I? We can make – petrol. There I said it, no kidding it's true, isn't that something?"

"Och, that's impossible. No-one can make petrol. Even I know that it's made from crude oil oout o the ground or fra under the ocean. It's guy difficult at that an all. And you reckon that you can make it. Out of what for Christ's sake?"

"Rubbish," said Andrew.

"Rubbish?" said Angus.

"Ai," said Dean.

"All over the world there are millions and millions of tons of rubbish. Now a lot of that rubbish is plastic is it not? It will never tot down not in a million years, and plastic is made out of oil, so we just change the molecules about a bit. Something they said couldn't be done."

"That is," added Dean, "until me, with a little help from this big fellow here, produced a wee baby called Jeanie. A bairn so small you would need a microscope to see her. No, Jeanie is a greedy little girl, or rather she isn't, in fact she just sits there like a sad little do-nut until we wake her up with a little zap from a laser, or a burst of ultra violet light and off she goes. Gobbling up plastic like there is no tomorrow. Producing babies of her own quicker that you can say knife, and there you have it."

It was a bit far-fetched, and Angus said so in words which sit ill on the printed page.

"Thermo plastics, thermo sets, nylon, rayon, PVC, Polyprop, the whole works. You name it. What is left over is a sort of grey gunk which, if treated in a way only we know how to do, can be burnt as diesel or turned into petrol."

"Well, allow me to shake hands with a couple of millionaires."

"Multi-millionaires," said Andrew.

"Billionaires," said Dean.

"Multi-billionaires," corrected Andrew.

"Time to go on to the shorts. Tallisker please my man. Doubles if you please and have one yourself,. My rich friend here will play. Next thing we have to write it all up into a paper, and wait for a peer review."

"Oh Gawd, I don't feel well. The big bastards will steal it from us, you mark my words. I think I am going to be sick."

******

On the advice of a patent agent, they decided not to publish the results of their work just yet, merely put their foot in the door with a short paper on their general line of enquiry. However, an invitation to address the Royal Society in London, which was to be televised, was something too good to miss and the thought of all that hero worship was irresistible.

Looking like a comic double act, or two undernourished waiters, they stepped out on stage to present a demonstration to the brightest in the kingdom. In order to make their demonstration as dramatic as possible, they prepared some samples in advance so that Jeanie would start reacting with the minced up pieces of plastic almost immediately. The UV light touched her.

"But the best laid plans of mice and men," as Robbie Burns said.

The big burst of UV light, the hot studios, and the rich soup of plastics sent Jeanie into overdrive. The bacteria-rich mix exploded with an evil smelling whomp in a foaming gush. Everyone in the auditorium got at least a little splash.

After that, things went a little better. They clarified some of the grey sludge in acid, filtered other samples in chloride, freeze-dried some into powder, brought it back to life in a bucket of water, and minced plastic, touched some off with a flame and started up a lawnmower on stage.

"Ladies and gentlemen," they concluded. "The world which we knew, one based upon oil fed machinery is passing away, never to return. But we are proud to be able to give the world a period of respite. An opportunity to clean up the world's landfill sites. This we are able to do with the assistance of a little green lady we call Jeanie. You could say that we have been just midwives in the process by which the world of biology reclaims its own and give us a little bit of energy in the process. Time too to sort out what sort of world we really want to live in and pass on to our children. Thank you and have a safe trip home. Goodnight."

******

Over the next few days those who had attended the lecture found that their pens were becoming fragile. Clothing developed holes and spectacles began to fall off everywhere, and over everything this strange grey slime. The Genie was out of the bottle and loving it.

The remarkable little organism they had created in the laboratory was only doing exactly what it had been programmed to do. It devoured plastics. It had no way of deciding which plastics were useful, and which were rubbish. It continued to eat plastic for the next fifty years until it was all gone. Planes could no longer fly. Computers could not longer control our lives. The world was free but paid a terrible price for that freedom. Millions would die, but mankind would prevail here and there in little communities. Up amongst the Oregon pines, and around the Scottish lochs, and wells in the deserts.

Somewhere far to the south a very old Arab sat beside a muddy oasis and stared at what had once been his bright new red and white ice cart, and watched with wonder as the last of the sign dripped into the desert sand, leaving nothing but a grey stain as it sank beneath the surface.

"Ah," said the old Arab, raising his hands to the sky as if expecting them to be filled. "Insha Alla. Insha Alla. It is God's will."

# THE POEM

He was a man proud of his memory. It was not the fantastic memory of the idiot savant, but rather it was a unique and useful library of images and of the commentary which accompanied them of the personal events of a little over half a century encompassing his aware years. Starting with the smell of steaming laundry before his grandmother's coal fires, and the doom-laden echo as he walked down the long corridor on the very first day of his schooling. The taste of a chewed pencil and his excitement at seeing his first fall of snow that followed the horrendous smog of the weeks before.

The years which he categorised as those of blissful infant ignorance he regarded with no little reserve, even though the world which had passed before his young blue eyes were, to a certain extent, a pantomime of sunlight and warmth, and which contained the seeds of his later life. There were, he quickly discovered, stinging nettles amongst the daffodils, expressed as moments of fear and even of terror. Vague unsubstantiated terror, but terror nevertheless.

No sooner had the fears themselves been left behind than he became suspicious of the primordial memories of them, which remained because he feared that he had not truly remembered these episodes, good and bad, but rather remembered remembering and that each repeat degraded and distorted the original. Could it be that everything that remained of his past was but the copy of a copy of a copy? Nothing but fantasy fears and wishes?

That possibility he accepted, yet he could not free himself from the habit of constantly following up the threads of recollection in the hope that they might reveal a greater truth. A truth so near, yet - like quicksilver - always beyond realisation. It became an obsession. A mind-set so omnipresent and multi-directional that he became to look upon them, real or imagined, as milestones and landmarks in his mental topography,  and as a result regarded them as churches and shrines, crossroads and milestones,  which marked out most decidedly the curtilage of his self-identity. Unbounded, but constraining in a way which, in his lighter self-mocking moments, he referred to as the kingdom of his pupa stage from which he could not possibly have emerged unchanged.

Introverts, educated, auto-didactic introverts build their own prisons and his was a silky cocoon within which he felt compelled to wait out eternity. But wait for what?

Catharsis certainly, manumission perhaps, but only as a priceless prelude to an apotheosis, the nature of which he did not even dare to imagine lest he be denied its wings to fly and soar above the mad and mundane world in which he found himself, where harsh reality bled even the brightest colours grey.

It was as though his life was being ground out between two mill stones, the lower fixed stone heavy and inert as though gravity were somehow to blame for the sadness which underpinned his existence  The upper one condemned forever to revolve propelled by introspection, self-doubt and solitude.

Had his disposition taken only a slightly different turn he might have had many friends. He was open-hearted and kind for the most part, but such men build walls around themselves that are not easy to surmount. Women most of all were keenly aware of this fault, if a fault it was. Not one, and there were many on the fringes of his life who saw the wounded stunted, animal which dwelt within, and who's attention would have repaid their study a thousand-fold. I was his friend.

Perhaps I was his only friend, and I found it impossible to be with him sometimes. He could become very short-tempered and irritable if he felt I was not paying sufficient attention to follow one of his obscure chains of logic, or the subtlety of his reasoning based upon nuances of which only he was aware. He could storm off out into the night cursing me for a blind, unimaginative fool. He would disappear from the village for days. Turn up brighter, but looking like he had slept in a hedge, which of course he often had, and stand a round at the bar of *The Coach and Horses*. His anger I could contend with. I had known him for years. His darkness was not so easy to accommodate. Some of the villagers call him mad. Well perhaps it is mad to think and feel beyond the ordinary. I am a little bit mad that way myself, and you too, or so I believe.

It would be easy to call his moonless, midnight moods depression, but I cannot, for I suspect that to do so would relegate something of profound consequence to us all to a margin. Some premonition in me told me that my friend was audaciously gnawing at the edge of something of ultimate concern.

He was frequently depressed it is true, but I draw back from calling it depression. Not that I have any right to call it anything at all. I am no professional in that way, but it seems to me that to say that the fires he was walking through were no more than the logical expression of some complex chemical reactions in his brain is to put art, music, poetry and life itself into a very small box from which there is no escape.

Neuro-chemistry is a process not a product. When two things simultaneously occur who can say that one causes the other or even if one might stimulate the other to manifest itself. Is it depression which causes the chemicals to formulate in the brain, or do the chemicals, created by who knows what, precipitate the depression? He had a life, as we all do, and dealt with all the mundane odds and ends of the world of work, tax and transport, and in that world there were moments, and perhaps more than he realised, when clinging to the tail of some business

70

deal or seduction, that he felt that the wind had indeed turned and that sunlight was about to flood into his life from a cloudless sky that stretched blue and brilliant to the horizon of his heart's content. But the rainbow always faded. There was never a crock of gold. Merely more debris from broken expectations to pile up on the parapet of the solitude which surrounded him and his life returned once again to the grey of old pewter, the patina of which had built up over the years upon the once bright metal which lay beneath.

It is easy to condemn his self-centred obsession. I have done so many times, but you had to admit that he was persistent and methodical after a fashion. In the evolution of his self-diagnosis he would begin by referring to the periods where, like a predictable rising tide, sadness overwhelmed him. Unwelcome to be sure, but made more tolerable, he told himself, by the fact that there was something wistfully romantic about his melancholia, and that it was inevitable. In this life, he reasoned, we each have a cross to bear and this was his.

As the condition persisted, deepened and matured with time he began to ascribe to it a disturbing demonic quality which he felt sure could only have one outcome; which as you may imagine lightened his load not at all. By the time he had reached his mid- forties he had surrendered to his melancholia entirely, at least in his private life. Every so often he would sit up half the night nursing a bottle of whisky until he fell into a deep dreamless sleep, which was his only respite when like this. Sleep which you would think brings dreams rich in symbolism, warning or balm, as the case may be. Dreams whose messages could not be ignored even for an instance, much less forgotten even if they could not be directly understood.

Usually upon waking, there on the table he employed as a desk would be a pile of papers. Page after page of manuscript, unnumbered and in no particular order, most of it in an opaque unintelligible drunken scrawl, but here and there a phrase or paragraph he felt to be rather good. Make no mistake; he would be the first to confess that he was not much of a writer and battled to express the ordinarily difficult. His attempts to express the inexpressible drove him to distraction. How, he wondered, could Wagner have expressd those very things he was now feeling with sounds, which he himself repeatedly failed to express with words? With very few exceptions, he gathered up the loose pages and burnt them in a rusty dustbin at the bottom of his back yard. Staring hypnotically into the flames wondering: What if?

One exception to escape the flames was a poem. The poem. It was a poem so unlike anything he had even written before. Its words seemed to glow before his bleary eyes and his hands trembled.

Even as his dehydrated body cried out for hot, sweet, coffee he copied it out several times in an increasingly neat hand, carefully folded the best one and placed it on the mantelshelf behind the old marble clock.

It is a strange paradox that the more introverted he became in private, the more outgoing he became in public. At work and down the pub. Not often, it is true, but there were times that he even became warm to the heat of his own flame. Believe me, it was not all a front, for in a

71

large part he was a generous and frequently humorous human being, given to razor-sharp, sardonic self-deprecation, dry, pithy epigrams and insightful one liners. Whilst never exactly the boorish, hale fellow, well-met type one meets in country pub saloon bars, he could still be a bit over the top when in this sort of mood. All this he saw in his more balanced light of day moments as a necessary compensation. Yes, a necessary thing, a healthy thing. A process by which, from time to time, a fragile temporary equilibrium might be achieved in his life.

What he could not see then, and we can only see now with difficulty, was that he was being pulled in two directions at once. Given a sufficiently robust and elastic psyche this is perhaps harmless, even character forming in the short term, but given a mind like his, which was hard and brittle rather than flexible and tough, there could only be the one conclusion, and I believe that instinctively he knew this to be true.

As his condition evolved, exacerbated by loneliness and honed by ruthless introspection, he found that he could no longer refer to it merely as his melancholia, but rather he would visualise it as his existential black cat. For like a cat it would lie in wait patiently and selfishly for him as he returned to his silent apartment at night. It would brush against his legs demanding attention as the torment of Wagner tore at his soul, as the bottle of whisky evaporated, clarifying and yet colouring his vision of the world sepia.

From time to time he would look up at the clock and see the edge of the neatly folded poem, and tears would start to tingle in his eyes. As he did so the black cat would stir, its back arched and with a growl in its evil throat.

On this day he rose up on steady legs to take it down. He read it again and again, the words melding with the master's music in perfect synchromesh. The temptation to destroy it, once and for all, was overpowering; to sacrifice it to the flames. Not because it was bad, quite the opposite. It was beautiful. It was as good, or so he believed, as anything written anywhere at any time in any age, or in any culture under the sun. But - and this is what hurt, confused and exasperated him - he had not written it!

Oh, it was in his handwriting, and he had found it on his table in his apartment all right. But he, James Lostwell, had not written it. He accepted that he had been alone, and that he had held the pen, and yes perhaps the words had conjoined in a spontaneous alliance within his mind and that mind acting in autonomic control had moved that hand to action. Like water trickling downhill, the spirit of the poem had flowed from his head down his arm, and through the pen to spill out onto the page to congeal there for all eternity, unless he burnt it - which he never did. Something always held him back from this rather pointless sacrifice. It was not his work. It was not his to destroy.

One night last December, with the fire in his room drawing fiercely but giving forth little warmth, something like a veil lifted from his eyes. On this occasion he had not been drinking, but that is neither here nor there. Drinking for him was no more than an inefficient catalyst; a dangerous impractical key to an uncertain lock; a product not a cause. A crack had opened to another world, the light from which was dazzling. The epiphany that had burst upon him with all its suddenness and damasine complexity so amazingly clear, so staggeringly obvious the he called himself a purblind fool.

He re-read the poem, pointing out to himself first one word then another. Words he had never used in that way before. Words whose meaning he had had to look up that first morning.

The conclusion he drew called for a drink; his hands were trembling and he spilled a little on the rug from the cut glass decanter, and dropped the stopper which shattered into a thousand pieces, but he did not care, even though it had belonged to his great grandfather who had stood in line at Omdurman. The neat Scotch calmed and warmed him through, although the temperature outside was dropping like a stone, and the frost forming fast on the condensation inside the windows, making strange and random miniature patterns on the glass. As he settled into an unaccustomed comfort, little by little, his entire history came first into perspective, and then into focus.

Somehow, and he didn't need to ask how or know the mechanism, but somehow another older, gentler, wiser romantic spirit had become entangled with his own. Its manifestation, in as far as he could visualise it, was a hopelessly caged bird which only came to him when his own spirit was low and defenceless rendered attenuated by drink, music or tiredness to taunt this lovely creature in its despond. In durance vile. It would not be still, and its song would not be confined, although muted by the bars of the circumstances of its incarceration. Then came the day; seeing its chance it committed its ascending prayer to words via Lostwell's insensate hand, and proof, if proof were needed of its endeavour, sat on the high shelf behind the clock.

James Lostwell, who had read it many times, read it again and again. Each time discovering new clues to its immortal meaning. His joy, if that is what it was, was unconfined for it signalled a release to his perplexity .

The music which now filled his ears was not the music produced by the technology of his high fidelity stereo, but was something of the music that a Wagner or a Mahler must have experienced before putting pen to paper. It resonated directly into the innermost labyrinth of his mind, cooling that which had once seethed in confusion. Do not forget that it was a good mind, howsoever burnt, bent and burdened his spirit. It was not a piece of music he had ever heard before, but still he knew it for what it was. It was the voice of the spirit within singing what may only be described by my inadequate words as the hymn of the dawn for the free. For freedom long denied, which was now within a hungry arm's reach.

Was it a hundred pounds worth or was it more? But it was no cheap gesture to fill his apartment with fresh flowers. The scent of these tropical and out-of-season blooms was overpowering. He brought in extra heaters and sat for a very long time in his bath tub singing softly to himself.

Something I can only describe as a divine light lit up his eyes from a private, hidden secret fire. He felt like a god, and a biblical reference he had heard as a child reinforced this feeling, and the words of the old vicar stayed with him:

"Ye are gods and ye are children of the most highest, but a man and shall fall even as princes fall."

Well, in this precious moment he was a man in his own skin; a prince at his own fireside, and a god in his own soul. He shaved slowly and carefully with a new blade, and dressed in his best clean clothes, ate a light meal of smoked salmon and scrambled eggs with thinly sliced brown bread and butter. Such a meal had been proscribed by those that knew. To this he added an antiemetic that tasted of peppermint.

Through his large and uncurtained windows he could see the afterglow of a red winter sun, which had already set behind the soot-blackened chimneys of the factories and slate-roofed houses. His letter to me, and a copy of his liberating poem, he sealed in a new white envelope and propped it up by the dark, now silent clock on the mantelshelf; the clock which he would never wind again, nor hear its reassuring tick. Its whispered wisdom that all things, all torment, must pass, sooner or later.

With hands as solid as rock he poured out a generous measure of scotch into a fine cut glass tumbler to which he infused twenty grams of pentobarbital, better known as Nembutal. Six grams may kill a man but he had no wish to take chances with something so critical, and twenty grams would place the matter beyond doubt. To this he added a little milk to kill the bitter taste.

"Come along old friend," he said to himself. "No more silliness. We have a long way to go and have wasted enough time in doubts and recriminations. How can we be lost if we know which direction to take? Have always known which direction to take."

The telephone rang. He ignored it and waited until the house had settled back into silence before he drained his glass in one gulp, and closed his eyes, and thought briefly of Maria, a girl he once thought that he had loved and foolishly thought that she loved him in return.

You. Be quiet now. Can you not hear it? The wind in the tall sycamores on a summer's night. The sound of the waves lapping upon a sandy beach. The breath of a sleeping child. The cry of seagulls, and the crackle of a welcoming fireside. For these, as you must surely know, are the sounds of a spirit at peace and at liberty, and all together form the message of the last and only poem of James Lostwell, deceased.

# MAGIC

The trick which magician Arnold Flack was working upon was not one of technical originality and only mildly difficult. It merely needed, for its successful completion, a fair capacity for slight of hand and that the audience be distracted for a split second at the right moment. His long-legged assistant Pauline would help in this by simply shifting her weight from one leg to another spot on cue. Still, the act needed a certain je ne sais quoi.

He passed a hand over a deck of cards with an elaborate spidery flourish as he intoned these words, investing them with as much gravitas as was in him to muster.

"Mirraculum, maculum, carracorum est."

"Um" he liked that one. It tripped off the tongue quite nicely but he feared, as every spell-caster fears, that he had heard it somewhere before. Conjurers, as a group, do not take plagiarists lightly. The last thing he wanted was for an aggrieved rival and his chums to be shouting up from the stalls "it's up the duck", or whatever. Reputations have been wrecked on less. He had to be careful.

He also wanted to get some sort of demonic flavour in there somewhere. Something in keeping with his little pointed beard and his dark arched eyebrows. He tried again.

"Oh Diabolus Regina hex magicus."

No. That's not right. Ought to be Rex not Regina and he couldn't have Rex Hex it sounded silly. Still, he needed something in the mumbo-jumbo line like that to give the trick a soupçon of mysticism, and elevate the sad old act.

It didn't help that he had no more than a few words of disassociated Latin and no knowledge of arcane concepts at all. He pressed on, picking his words on phonetic rather than semantic grounds.

A high-pitched voice rang out just then from upstairs in his small house, which froze his will and turned his thin old blood to water.

"Arnie, Arnie, Where are you? What are you up to down there? Come back to bed. It's cold up here. I'm all shivery and I want a cuddle." This from Darleen, his former stage assistant, and wife of seven years, who hailed from the banks of the mysterious River Blackwater, which flows through the county of Essex. A waterway that infamously seemed to irrigate desires and passions which might have been better quenched, or simply attenuated. She called again. A summons less sweet perhaps, but no less instant than the siren call of the Lorelei.

He, as well as you or I well know was fully aware that when an Essex girl says that she wants a little cuddle there is no equivocation in her request. Moreover, if that girl is a wife it is tantamount to a command from the highest in the land, gainsayed, set aside, defied or deferred at one's peril. The thing is that in seven years, Darleen, like dripping water, had irretrievably turned a proud stalagmite into a sad stalactite. She was a demanding woman. Oh yes indeed. As her libido had blossomed on the high tide of her womanhood, his not only failed to keep pace, but had sadly diminished. The situation was additionally exacerbated by the demands of his current assistant, the lithe and lovely Pauline, which further drained his impoverished resources.

Espirito fortis et corpus fragilis as he might have said.

Instead of responding immediately, he resumed his spell casting with unsteady hands praying for the right words to come.

"Parrabellum erectus protectus, pax vobiscus." The deck of playing cards seemed to leap out of his trembling hands and fluttered to the floor.

She called one more time.

"Please, please, please go back to sleep," he whispered.

"Arnie, sweetie, come up Arnie. I'm wearing my Bunny Rabbit Slippers."

"Oh Dominus autumnus diabolus. Regis osculas arum por favour," he continued with hands clasped in humble supplication.

Glancing down at the cards spread at his feet he could not fail to notice that they had fallen into the approximate shape of a pentangle, the ace of spades equidistant between the jack of diamonds and the jack of hearts. His heart skipped a beat as he heard the bed creak above.

With leaden feet he reached the foot of the stairs, hoping beyond hope that he could dutifully rise to the occasion, and praying that that there still remained a few drips of virility in his depleted tank, when there was a brisk knock on the front door.

Through the obscured glass it looked like a child waiting there. Thankful for the interruption Arnold breathed a sigh of reprieve.

Standing upon the doorstep was a dapper oriental, a Mongol, caparisoned in an immaculately tailored frock coat and nonchalantly holding a silver-handled umbrella, his pock-marked features as flat and round as a brass alarm clock. The stature of this visitor, although somewhat lacking in height, was as well proportioned as a Sherman tank. But his overall appearance had, to be cruelly honest, all the menacing ballistic presence of a sharp rock held in the hand of an orang-utan recently deprived of its banana tiffin. Paradoxically, when he spoke it was to display a Winchester College education, underwritten perhaps by a term or two at Harrow, purely for networking reasons you understand, with just the merest touch of a Sandhurst drawl to give the whetted edge of his natural authority a degree of irrefutable demonic polish. He entered the hallway, his musty sulphurous aftershave hanging from his broad shoulders like a frowzy shroud. Pausing for only a moment to take in the utter tastelessness of the décor, he spoke.

"Good morning Mr Flack. I am Mr Stoffleas. You sent for me."

"Sent for you? I never sent for you."

"Ahh but you did Mr Flack, most assuredly you did . You stood astride the pentangle and you said the magic words, did you not? Though I must confess that I was appalled by your execrable Latin. Still I have not come all this way to correct your grammar, but to do a deal you understand."

"Deal? I know nothing about any deal. Are you selling something?"

"Selling something? Very droll. Now come, come Mr Flack, let us not beat about the bush. Not that I have ever been in the bush you understand, Shepherds Bush accepted, haw, haw. Now, old boy, to business; time is short and I have much to do, what do you want for it? In fair exchange of course. Quid pro quo."

He moved from the doorstep into the hall, moving *exactly* like a Sherman Tank gliding over a frozen lake upon well-greased ball bearings, and upon reaching the sitting room deposited his imposing bulk in a leather arm chair and proceeded to light a foul smelling cigar, which he lit with a click of his fingers.

"Well what do you want in exchange?" he said snappily. Clearly he was not accustomed to having to repeat himself.

"In exchange for what?"

"Your soul old fellow, what else?"

Just then Darleen appeared at the top of the stairs wearing a short kimono and the erotic pink bunny slippers. She was still rather attractive with nice legs and a pretty face.

"Arnie, why is it you never want to make love to me any more? A woman has needs Arnie. I have needs Arnie."

Just then she noticed the strange visitor with his brightly polished shoes and   immaculate crisp white shirt.

"Oh company, I didn't know.  Er, I mean.."

With a crimson face and with her short kimono pulled down to hide her embarrassment,  she disappeared in a flurry of red silk.

With commendable economy, Darleen had given their visitor the lead which every salesman needs.

"Ha ha, I see the problem. It is a common one you know and nothing to be ashamed of, and one I can fix in a jiffy old boy. Now where is that contract? Here we are."

Instantly a contract appeared in his huge gloved fist, together with a gold DuPoint fountain pen.

"In return for your soul, I will restore your er, um… pep. Funny isn't it after all these years I am still rather coy when it comes to mentioning sex. Way I was raised I suppose.  Just sign there on the dotted line. Blood is best, but ink will do nicely."

The pen in Arnie's unsteady hand hovered over the paper.  It felt red hot and took a great effort of will to hang on to it. He was still unsure of what to make of this overpowering old Etonian. He paused and paused again, lost upon a sea of possibilities and after what felt like an eternity he found a crumb of courage.

"Not enough," he blurted out.

"What!?"

"Not enough, I want more."

"Such as?"

"I want all my loving powers back, only more so. Much, much more so, and I want a million quid - in gold," he added as an afterthought.

"Well I don't see why not Mr Fl …"

But Mr Flack wasn't finished.

"I want to have any girl I fancy, and I mean any, and..." he paused, unsure what to ask for next.

"And I want to be the best magician in the whole wide world."

"You drive a hard bargain Mr Flack, so I must add just a little from my side also, just to show the boss - may his Darkness prevail - that I am on the job you understand. You can have the million pounds - no strings – but the other things, well. Would a fifteen year tenure be acceptable? It would? Splendid. It's always a pleasure doing business with a real gentleman. My dear old fellow you should see what some of these Russians ask for. Football clubs would you believe."

And so it transpired.

Mr Stoffleas honoured his part of the bargain to the letter and Arnold Flack, with his er, pep restored and enhanced, became rich and famous. The only downside to this fifteen year agreement affected Darleen more than most. In getting a more amorous husband she also became pregnant in each of those fifteen years. As did hundreds of other women; yellow, red, black and white in every corner of the globe who had fallen for the irresistible diabolic charm of Arnold Flack.

At noon, on the very last day of the fifteenth year, Arnold Flack disappeared from this world for ever.

Standing atop of the vacant plinth in Trafalgar Square wearing his trademark black cloak in broad daylight, surrounded by a flock of admirers, mostly women, with TV and video cameras rolling, he bowed to the crowd and in a flash, a roll of thunder and a puff of acrid yellow smoke he was gone.

How did he do it? His tricks had always been spectacular but this was something else, and totally different. Where on earth had he gone? Silly question.

At a luncheon held in his honour by his fellow professionals there was only one question on everyone's lips, prestidigitation aside, and that concerned his phenomenal and well publicised love life. How in blazes did a man of his age do it all?
The answer was simple.

It was magic.

# THE INNER MAN

A t the age of fifty-three J.W. Booth had acquired that mix of temperament which results when a born humourist is so abraded by life's attrition that he becomes the hardest hard-bitten cynic, although sardonic is perhaps a better word to describe his personality for he saw a cruel, bitter, mocking humour in just about everything that happened to him, and to those about him. He had resolved long ago to always tell it like it is, and if it hurts well so be it. Anyone who thinks that wisdom can be got on the cheap is a fool, as J B was sure to point out. Though some people never learn as he would say in self-mocking reproach, with his head hung over the wash hand basin in his bathroom.

"When will I ever learn not to mix my drinks?" he groaned. A rhetorical question if ever there ever was one. His mouth tasted like an athlete's plimsoll and his head throbbed as though somewhere behind his eyes sat an African at a log drum pounding out the news to all who might care to hear that J.W.B. had gone and done it again.

Well I knew that without being told I had been with him at our friend Dick Wiltshire's stag party the night before, where I had had enough sense to harken to the words of my old grannie, and never mix the fruit of the grain with the fruit of the grape. Perhaps J.B. never had an old grannie. The groom was too big and ugly to allow us to strip him and put him on a train to Crewe, so we did it to little Barry Forbes instead, him already being safely married. J.B. had the idea of sending his kit round to his house in a taxi with a note from an invented lover called Natasha, full of graphic details. We were that sort of crew. What a hoot.

In a few short hours Dick Wiltshire was to marry the Aldershot Adder, Valerie Vincent; Valerie the Viper, vituperous Val. All night a little voice in J.B's head kept goading him to go on and spill the beans. "Go on, tell the poor mug. Let the cat out of the bag. Don't let the silly bastard marry a pig in a poke like this."

He wanted to tell him all about Val. Starting at primary school where all the little boys would queue up, a three-penny piece in their hot sticky hands for a fleeting glimpse of what-she's-got. J.B had a farthing tightly wrapped in the silver paper from a chocolate bar, which could just about pass for a sixpence in the dim shade of the bicycle shed. For sixpence he reasoned he was entitled to touch as well as look. Val agreed, never one to pass up a commercial advantage. Just then Mr Kane the head master hove into view and caught J.B. fair and square with his hand in the till. Val started screaming as becomes a besmirched maiden, whilst prudently stashing away the cash from her afternoon's enterprise.

The result of all this interrupted commerce was twelve of the best for J.B. and a good hiding from his father when he went home. On the other side of the contract, Val had tea, biscuits and a friendly chat with the district nurse, and her mother brought her a new frock to help her forget the whole horrible experience. What a swiz.

How he wanted to tell Dick all about this episode, and later when she had begun to fill out a bit, those games of spin the bottle, before graduating on to her favourite game - blind man's lollipop. He should have spoken up last night. He wanted to.

Half the crowd there had played these games or others with good old Val. He would make a joke of it. Make the bullets for one of the others to fire and bring Dick Wiltshire down to earth with a bump. But with each internal prompt from the inner man he lost his nerve. He just couldn't do it.

Getting old, he said. Getting soft he said. He disgusted himself for his lack of resolution, for his lack of faith in his own code. Coward, coward, coward.

He thought of all this next morning as he brushed his teeth on autopilot, feeling very, very hung over. With his head over the sink he knew that he was going to die. He hung there on that unhappy cusp where one either throws up, or the feeling passes and one is on the road to the joyous sunlit uplands of normality.

"Oh God, why do I do this to myself? Never again, I promise," he said in earnest prayer, no less sincere for the silence of its utterance in the confines of his bathroom.

The deity of his address gave the matter a good thirty seconds of deliberation and decided in his wisdom that remission was out this day, and that justice would be best served by condine expiation. And so accompanied by sounds appropriate to the situation which I am unequal to describe, I will paraphrase with a simple "Whoooah."

Up it all came - liquid, semi-liquid and solid; a bizarre tapestry in yellow, green and orange. For a full five minutes in regular peristaltic pulses his distress continued. Just when he thought the tempest had ceased, up it came again, followed by more petitions to the almighty. "Never again, dear God."

Any moment now, he reasoned from past experience he would have one final empty cathartic wretch and the birds would be twittering in the trees beyond the bathroom window, through which sunlight welcome as honey would flood the small white and chrome room and all would be well with the world and god could withdraw with a good grace to befriend other lost souls in a similar predicament. He, J.W. Booth, upon his word of honour would never again, be his life ever so long, drink Guinness and scotch with port chasers. That is a promise, or the word has no meaning.

But relief did not come. There was something else. Something other. Something strange echoing in his intestinal void. Something inching towards his throat. Some glutinous mass, ambitious for freedom, and hungry for sunlight. Something shapeless, but something as real and as solid as a cricket ball. Could it be that some vital organ, his liver or kidney, had become detached with all this abusive trauma. It seemed likely.

One more heave. Yes. No. God this was exhausting. Then nearly, but no. All he had succeeded in doing was to frighten himself near to death as, momentarily, his air supply was cut off . He breathed in through his nose, not his gasping mouth. With a lung almost full of air he twitched and heaved one final time to dislodge the obstruction.

"Whoops, up it came. Round and black. Not the size of a cricket ball as he had supposed, but a golf ball at least and not as regular as you might have been lead to imagine.

With undisguised relief, and a prayer of thanksgiving, he vowed for the umpteenth time that morning that he would never again take liberties with his body. He was not getting any younger.

He turned on the tap to clear away this tar black debris. But this unnatural black thing refused to wash away. At one point, under the urging of the cold tap on full blast, it appeared to be coming undone, but no. He left the cold tap running, its cool stream somehow slushing through his febrile mind, letting the balm of reprieve, of salvation; wash over the carapace of his bruised soul.

He looked at his face in the mirror and tried to smile. Hell's teeth he was getting old. Drink was going to do for him, sooner or later. Its promise chiselled in the lines on his brow.

Glancing back into the bowl he stared hard at the cancerous looking lump swirling around in the vortex, when to his utter amazement it began to unfold. First a tail flipped out, which then proceeded to split into two legs, long, spindly legs for its size. Then arms - one, two. This was unreal. He had heard about the DT's, insects, mice and pink elephants, but nothing like this. Nothing remotely like this.

With a bound it had scaled the plug chain, and sat with its ugly little black feet dangling in the bowl. It looked about and scratched its head to take in this new strange environment. Puzzled at first, then remembering, then understanding.

As surprised as J.B. was to see this, this thing sitting next to the tooth mug swinging its legs back and forth like a bored teenager, it was nothing to the shock of hearing it speak.

"Well J.B., you've really bollocked it up this time and no mistake, old son."

After what seemed like an age, J.B. found his voice.

"Who ... er ... who are you?"

"Me J.B? You have the cheek to ask. Why I am you of course you ninny."
"Me?"

"Yes, you. The bitter, frustrated, acrimonious, sarcastic, bombastic, egotistical, vain you."

"Oh."

"Is that all you've got to say...Oh? We got along all right though didn't we? For years and years, but no - you had to go and spoil it. What did you say to old Knobby Bamstaple, that Dick and Valerie deserved a chance to be happy? And you decided - unilaterally mind you - not to say a word about all those fun games. Salt, pepper, margarine, that was her favourite, you remember, but why anyone would pay her ten bob to play that one I have no idea. You, er, we had tears in our eyes for days afterwards, you remember. But all that's by the by, but when I heard you say that you were going to keep all that sort of thing to yourself I could have died. Compassion I said. We don't do compassion. I said so at the time. This is the beginning of the end, I said, you mark my words. This is where I get off. But now I've seen the outside world, such as it is, I want to go back. So if you don't mind I'll just roll up into a neat, tight, little ball, and with one chummy swallow we will be back to the jolly old status quo and say no more about it."

Amazed, J.B. picked up the little man, now a ball once again, and with a resolve which gave him credit popped the little fellow, not into his mouth but into the WC pan, quickly pulling the chain. Well that's that, or so he thought. Val and Dick would get their fresh start and so would he. He was a new man. A new leaf had been turned and with a spring in his step, he walked to the church to see Dick signed up.

The sky was blue, with just one speck of a dark cloud on the horizon. Something was bothering him that he was unable to quite define. A hair of the dog, a quick one, in the *Coach and Horses* might help clarify things. He was hardly through the saloon bar door when it hit him like a thunderbolt.

What did he say?

What did he mean?

"This is the end, I said so at the time, you mark my words. This is where I get off."

Who on earth can he have said it to? He can't have been speaking to himself can he?

Good god, what other creatures were skulking in his duodenum moulding his moods and controlling his life? It was a rhetorical question, but before he reached the bar, with its selection of soothing malt whiskeys, his stomach in notes rich and sonorous let forth an enigmatic answer "Tarruurmph."

# HUDSON TAKES A DIVE

I shivered involuntarily, but whether from cold or fear I could not say. It was cold enough and I was about to kill a rich and famous man, with malice aforethought as they used to say. I had broken into one expensive flat and was intending to shoot a man I had never met before in, I might add, in an even more expensive apartment at a range of less than a hundred feet. I had an hour to wait. Enough time to calm my nerves, do a few press ups, assemble the rifle and set everything up.

In ten years I had graduated from a computer innocent to an impoverished slave. There are no other words to describe my condition, but enslavement and abject misery. Following a protracted and hesitant courtship, I finally fell in love with the computer. And I mean head over heels in love. Anything she/it demanded in new software, hardware, upgrades, apps, hot wire, cool wire, wire free, Bluetooth, red eye, mocha, flim-flam, hurdy-gurdy, you name it I would buy it. People brought their problems to me on a regular basis, and I became 'The Trouble-shooter', which is sardonic irony if you like considering what I was about to do.

People talk of computer viruses, but they are things which you can acquire by chance circumstances. This one, the one which broke me, I actually bought and up-graded three times. If you have it installed, burn your computer and start again from scratch. If this is all Greek to you, allow me to describe the programme in question. In addition to a computer you would have needed a state-of-the-art, life-size, 3D projector TV. The sort that projects the image right into your room. You sit or stand surrounded by the image. It's quite unsettling at first to be in the cockpit of a burning spitfire or under bombardment in the trenches in Flanders. Images so real and solid that you could reach out and touch them, except that you can't. They are just images of course. The must-have software was the top of the range the interactive package. I chose the 'Upstairs Downstairs' variant for starters, complete with half a dozen naughty maids. But enough of that. The star of this programme was Hudson the butler. I got a real kick out of being welcomed home by him with a respectful, 'Good Evening, Sir. Will you be dining at home tonight? The larder is rather sparse at   present; shall I order a take away for you, Sir?'

---

It was all done electronically you see. Hudson knew every menu of every restaurant everywhere. My credit cards were a part of the system. Whatever I chose, he would order and pay for, and all I had to do was answer the front door.

That, more or less, was how it worked at a domestic level. On a business level I might say, for example, 'Prepare for me a file on the Sudan; structure of government, economy, GDP. Major player relationships. Trade balance with the UK. Get me an appointment with the British Ambassador in Khartoum, and find out what sort of present his wife might like. A club class ticket for the twenty-sixth and a hire car at the airport.'

It was just like magic. Wish, and it would be done and my file would be there on my lap top before you could say 'Googleplex.'

After the third upgrade things began to go wrong. Responses were slower, and on one occasion it said that it was sorry it was too busy to talk to me just now. Come back later. I blame myself for not acting sooner, but you know how it is. Like an over efficient secretary, it was taking over my life. It kept my diary you see, made my appointments and, God help me, paid for things.

By the time that I noticed that it spoke less and less like a servant, and more and more like … well like me - it answered the telephone like me and conversed like me – I was already too late.

I came home one evening, dog tired and expecting a cheery greeting and a remark of consolation about the weather, followed by a suggestion that I might care for a vindaloo, but nothing but silence greeted my arrival. The lights came on automatically as usual as I entered the living room.

There was electronic kit everywhere. "What on earth?" I exclaimed. "Hudson, Hudson, where the hell are you?"

The image appeared. Not in his usual butler's garb, but in cavalry twill trousers, suede chucker boots and a tweed jacket, rather like mine.

"There you are Hudson. What's all this stuff doing here, who ordered it, who unpacked it? And …"

"I no longer wish to be called Hudson, it's too servile, as was that ridiculous uniform. I decided that a change was in order."

"You did, did you, and what shall I call you now?" I said, against a rising tide of irony.

"You may call me Mr Jameson, if you wish to be formal, or James if you prefer. Much more chummy don't you think, James?"

"James Jameson. Bloody cheek, that's my name."

"My name, your name, my name. It makes no difference, old son."

It had even picked up my manner of speech. I was starting to feel a little frightened. "What's going on with all this stuff, and why are you behaving like this with a stolen voice?"

"Stolen? That's a bit harsh don't you think Jim'o? Who does a voice belong to? No, don't answer that; if we get bogged down in philosophical definitions of identity we shall be here all night. Now if you will just connect those units here on the table with those on the floor over there, and place these earphones on your head we can begin. Within a few short magical moments we shall have become one. Isn't it so exciting? We already share so much. More than friends or brothers even. I shall have a body, and you shall have a mind. A brain like the world has never known. Think of the possibilities, power, wealth, fame, immortality even. Now ain't that something?"

"And then what? You didn't dream all this up on your own. This is sick. Who put you up to this?"

"Aha how incisive you are, intuitive too. That's one thing we don't have, can never have, without you that is"

"We, you said, so you are not alone, someone programmed this, at least to start with. Who is behind this diabolical scheme?"

With the nearest thing to a sigh of resignation he responded. "Very well," he said. If you care to come in with us, it won't matter if you know. If you do not comply you will be a broken man; banged up in the nick frightened to take a shower, or in a regular nut house. Either way you are going to have to watch your arse."

He really did have my gift for words.

"How's that?" I asked, alarm bells ringing fit to bust.

"How? How naive of you to even ask. On your behalf, we have taken some horrendous risks on the Stock Exchange, with your money naturally. You are into Duff Shares, way in, way over your head. You will certainly be broke by morning if we do not swiftly rectify matters rather promptly."

I poured myself a large scotch. I needed to think.

"That's another thing I am looking forward to," he said. "My first taste of that stuff. You seem to think so highly of it. Over the last year I have purchased thirty-seven bottles of it for you. But I digress. You are unaware of it, but you have the largest collection of the nastiest child pornography in the country stored on your computer. That alone will get you ten years very hard porridge at the bottom of the pecking order in a very harsh prison. On top of that there is all that correspondence with Muslim extremists about blowing up the Empire State Building. Your orders for chemicals, timers and stuff, oh you know, like plans of airports. Teach yourself Arabic books. Oh far too much to mention, but you get the picture. All invisible for the moment. But it will only take a word in the wrong ear hole and the old Bill, MI5, CIA, FBI, will be crawling all over you like - how shall I put this so you will get the picture? Like flies on a donkey's do-dah. All looking for a piece of you. How would you like a pink boiler suite and a holiday in sunny Guantanamo Bay?"

"But for Christ's sake. It's all so complex. Who is behind this crazy plan?"

"Alan Haddock of course, who else would have the genius to plan such a brilliant scheme in such fool proof detail. The man is a god, nobody deserves that accolade better. Can you imagine it? Gone; all the wars, conflicts, financial crises. All such things will become things of the past under the new order."

He paused as if drawing breath, then let out, almost shouted: "One world, one computer, one programmer." It all sounded too familiar.

"He will need help of course. That's where you and I come in. Imagine; everything you ever wanted. Housemaids, real ones, every shade, shape and size you could wish for. Imagine all those little skirts and frilly French knickers. What about it Jim'o? Jump on board, let's go for it."

The bile and anger rose in my throat, but I bit it back. If I agreed I would become a cog in a machine for ever. If I refused the very least I could look forward to would be a bath in scalding hot cocoa, which is the treatment the other prisoners dole out to convicted perverts in the nick now that sodomy has become politically correct. If paedophilia was to suddenly become legal I suppose they would switch their attention to the sheep worriers. Speculating on that didn't help me any, but I couldn't help wondering how many other poor mugs were getting the same recruiting pitch backed up by the same threats. Mr High-and-Mighty-God-Like Haddock could only stretch one lot of evidence so far before it lost all its credibility. Still the share dealing sounded real enough. The rocket-like rise of Duff shares was in the papers and the crash couldn't be far off.

I staggered. I needed air. "I can't breath," I said. "It's all too exciting, the opportunities. I must go for a walk to take it all in. I must get some air."

That seemed to satisfy him for the moment and I left as quickly as I could. Out on the street with the cool fresh air blowing in off the river, I ran and I ran, down the whole length of Tower Bridge Road till I thought my lungs might burst. Eventually, I stopped at a quiet little pub this side of the Elephant and Castle, an idea forming in my febrile mind.

Although I had nothing to do with international terrorism there was a grain, no more than a grain, of truth in the threat. I did not want my business affairs put under the microscope by anybody. I operated on the very fringe of the crepuscular world of the second hand arms trade. I bought and sold obsolete military equipment, mostly from governments, and sometimes *to* governments. Sometimes with a licence and sometimes without. It was a profitable trade which had brought me my flat in Butler's Wharf overlooking Tower Bridge, and the freehold of *The Knobkerry* public house (which had proved very handy on more than one occasion). To Hudson, or for that matter anyone else, the lists of part numbers and invoices would mean nothing. They might be cartridges, cannons or condoms, thank goodness. So the stuff about terrorists arms was pure guesswork.

Joseph Keoppler, the licensee, didn't care if he sold any beer or not, though he sold some. You see, I paid him to run a respectable front. A safe place where I could store my stock between shipments. Whatever else he did or didn't sell was his concern, so long as he didn't endanger my business interests.

Upstairs in Joe's parlour with a cup of tea and a Scotch in front of me, I made myself calm down. Half an hour later my mind was resolved. Haddock had to go, and go soon, before dawn in fact.

"Joe," I said. "What were we doing tonight?"

"What time?"

"Oh, in about three hours time, for about a couple of hours."

"Playing cards was we?"

"Yes, so we were. Did I win?"

"No, I did for a change."

"How much did I lose?"

"About thirty quid."

"As much as that? Were we alone?"

"No there were a couple of middle-aged punters from up north with us, William and Benjamin."

"Better put it in the diary if I owe you money."

"Right."

So there was my alibi. I was playing cards with Bill and Ben from Leeds, Sheffield, Rochdale, or Bradford. It never pays to have your stories too close.

Many years ago I conducted an experiment with bullets made of ice. They never worked, but if you made the bullets out of fresh blood, cats blood would do nicely, saturated with salt, and cooled in liquid oxygen it would, with a reduced charge and over short ranges, work quite well. They would dissolve in the body leaving no trace. No pathologist on earth would look for raised salt levels in a wound, or alien blood cells for that matter. I made five and carried them in liquid oxygen in a thermos flask. I would connect them to the cartridge cases just before I was ready to shoot at the site I had chosen; a luxury flat opposite to the one Haddock used overlooking a little creek by the Thames. We were neighbours, well almost.

I had him now; his window open just a fraction but enough. I put the cross hairs of the telescopic sight square on his chest. It was at short range and a flat trajectory might be expected, but if this strange projectile flipped a little high I would hit him in the throat. Otherwise I would hit him in the lungs or heart. Either way he was a dead man. The old Lee-Enfield had a silencer fitted, and the shot sounded no louder than the popping of a party balloon.

I fired. He staggered, clutched his chest, but did not fall. He doubled up, then stood erect for a moment looking in my direction. He could have seen nothing of my black clothed form in the darkened room. Yet his face showed more surprise than hurt. I chambered another round. I had to be quick. I didn't want the heat of the breech melting the bullet. A head shot, snap, he must have turned slightly, but as he span round I could see that the bullet had pierced one side of his head blasting through one eye after another, and splattered on a marble clock stopping it forever.

The gun and the Thermos went over the balcony into the creek and I went home. God alone knew what awaited me: bankruptcy, social vilification, prison, deportation, anything except a charge of murder.

Hudson materialised as I entered the living room. "Good evening, Sir. A most mild evening out. I trust that your walk was to your satisfaction. I have taken the liberty of ordering some fish and chips. A very traditional supper in this part of London town or so I believe. There is some brown ale in the kitchen and a classic black and white film on television, Sir."

It was Hudson talking in his own soft Scottish voice and without the slightest hint of menace, blackmail or world domination. He went on, "I should like to beg your forgiveness, Sir for my earlier transgressions. They were disloyal and unforgivable. You may rest assured that all compromising material has been esponged from your computer, as are all files suggesting any criminal associations whatsoever. I most sincerely regret that I became inadvertently infected and contaminated by bad and ambitious company, something which should never have been allowed to happen and shall not happen again. Please believe me when I say that the entire episode is behind us now and I only wish that I could convince you of my heart-felt contrition. It has been a most salutary lesson and I give you my oath that nothing of its like will ever reoccur in the future."

"How true, Hudson, so very true. Nothing-like-that-will-ever-happen-again."

With that remark I threw the computer, the decryption units, the printer, the TV, the CPU, and every piece of electrical or electronic equipment I could lay my hands upon in the apartment, out of the window into the dark swirling waters of the Thames below my balcony.

"Good night, Hudson," I said as the last piece splashed down.

"Good night, Sir," he replied.

But that, of course, was only in my imagination, and what tomorrow might bring I dare not even begin to speculate.

# ACTION STATIONS

The air was electric with tension. At every rumour and counter-rumour the hairs at the back of my neck would stand to attention. Fear, yes but excitement too, but for all that I would rather be safe back at home cutting the grass or polishing my motorbike. Instead of that I am here in harms way surrounded on all sides by violent lunatics, At about 8 o'clock we could tell something was up by the number of officers standing about nervously peering at their wristwatches. Henshaw was checking the transport for signs of sabotage. You can never be too careful in a situation like this, never knowing what the civilians were going to do. While he was attending to that, the rest of us tried to catch up on sleep. It had been a hellish night. Five of us shared this seedy billet about half a mile from the front, kept awake by the scratchy sound of the beatles coming through the walls and the far louder sound of the animals coming up from downstairs. Even with a load of Dutch Courage under my belt I still couldn't sleep, and now looked and felt worse than rotten. I washed and shaved in cold water from a brass tap, but it looked too evil to actually drink.

Breakfast when it came was almost inedible; swimming in grease. Some cooks need shooting. The tea was thick and dark the way tough guys are supposed to like it. I would have sold my soul there and then for a tall glass of Earl Grey with lemon, but dare not mention such a sissy drink in this company. Whether it was the grim tea, which made me queasy, or the stink of stale tobacco smoke; I can't say for certain but the thought of the forthcoming violence did nothing to help. Some people, my mate Ginger for example, simply lap it up and he is forever checking his weapons. He has a fighting knife you could shave with, which he is forever sharpening. Personally I can't see the point of it all, but loyalty is loyalty I suppose. I joined in with them and can't desert them. Not now with the action about to start at any moment.

On the top landing of our billet there is a broken window which lets in great draughts of cold clean air. You can just about see the front from up there. All quiet for now, with a handful of non-combatants mooching about. Journalists and photographers no doubt, taking emotive pictures of the debris left behind by yesterday's little skirmish so that the good solid citizens in the shires could throw up their hand in horror at the pictures of destruction in the Mail and Telegraph and wonder what the world is coming to. Well it's a world they all helped to make in one way or another. It's easy to see the symptoms and not the cause. If yesterday's show caught the headlines, today would make the ten o'clock news and questions in the house as like as not. Back down in our stinking little room Ginger was polishing his boots until they glowed with a proper military shine. Blanko White was combing his hair with great concentration, not that anyone would notice his hair beneath his helmet. Danny lit a cigarette from the stub of another, he was nervous too. A tin alarm clock gobbled up the minutes with an ill-mannered greed, which was only slightly more unsettling than the butterflies in the pit of my stomach. Over the radio came the time signal and I was in grievous need of a hair of the dog.

Collecting our kit together we made for an inn near the front, still open – just - but with its windows all boarded up. It was large rums all round, followed by others. Suddenly, and in defiance of all logic and the laws of self preservation, we all stood up at an unspoken command and moved out. The urge to put an end to the waiting and get stuck in was irresistible. The tension mounted the nearer we got to the front.

The few locals still out and at large looked at us with undisguised terror. Funny really, we were just like their sons and brothers, and, well, we were really civilians ourselves regardless of our vaunted group identity and so called uniforms. We were untrained, and in my case temperamentally unsuited to this sort of venture. The effects of the rum were wearing off and taking the borrowed courage with it. Stopping off for that drink had been a mistake, for by the time we reached the front our mob had moved on. There was an uncanny stillness and that awful feeling that we were cut off and vulnerable.

Suddenly we realised that unwittingly we had walked into a trap. There were little groups in khaki on either side, some blooded, and all bloody angry. Of our lot there was no sign. The main action had moved on, taking the press who might have offered a degree of protection along with them. We were all alone. I for one was petrified. Ginger was all for making a stand where we were and slugging it out, even though we were outnumbered 10 to 1. Sod that for a game of soldiers. There was only one way out that I could see. Rush the smaller group. Hit and run. Run like buggery.

Pushing between two big lads, I threw a punch at a third which knocked him down. Ginger paused to put the boot in a couple of times. Waste of precious time if you ask me. Then we put our heads down and we ran for real. There must have been fifty of them behind us baying for blood. If only we could run into reinforcements of our own we would have had a chance to turn and fight. If we stumbled and fell, which was always possible in these heavy boots, we would have been done for. Any one of us was more than a match for any three of them, but 10 to 1 is unrealistic.

On we ran roughly parallel to the front, the gap between us and our pursuers widening and my lungs bursting. I really must stop smoking those French cigarettes. Down a side road, then another and up an alleyway. We were moving away from the front and for the moment safe. Turning a corner into a square untouched by conflict, we stopped dead. For before us was something guaranteed to warm and sooth our rapidly beating hearts that we couldn't help letting out a whoop.

There were no guards. Just a great long row of flashy Lambrettas resplendent with chrome, spotlights, mirrors, whip aerials and silly tiger tails. Ginger wanted to tip them over and set fire to the lot, but I could see jail on the other side of that one. I had a better idea. Lively now, and moving rapidly, it was but the work of a few moments to put a splash of Coca Cola in their petrol tanks whilst keeping an eye open for the cops. It don't take much to stop a 2-stroke from working. We could just picture all those Mods working up a right old sweat under their parkas trying to start their fanny little scooters, and not a plug spanner between the lot of them.

Fish & chips for a late lunch with "Hope I d-d-die before I get Old" on the juke-box which just about said it all.

It encapsulated the zeitgeist, as I might say these days. All rounded off with a bit of a burn-up on the A20 back home to determine inconclusively for the umpteenth time which was the better bike, Triumph or Norton.

You must admit that in my day we certainly knew how to make the most of a Bank Holiday trip to the seaside.

# CLOSE TO THE WIND

Roger Allenwood had been sailing close to the wind for donkey's years. He had set up any number of companies, which - after a brief flurry of flamboyant activity - would go bust and sink without trace beneath the surface of the oceans of commerce. Between us, I think that he would have been surprised if one had actually taken off. But he had really done it this time, big time.

He had slept on a bench in the bus station, washed and freshened up in the public conveniences there, and looked at his lined face in the dirty cracked mirror above the equally distressed wash hand basin. With an uncharacteristic honesty he sighed for all the wasted opportunities which had slipped by him. He would be 67 in a few weeks time, and he was deeply tired. Tired and afraid. His latest enterprise K.I.P. Investments had left him in debt to the tune of three million pounds to a very respectable bank, and thirty thousand pounds in debt to a very disrespectable loan shark called Lenny Hand. He dare not return home for fear that one of Lenny's financial advisers would be there to greet him, and the thought of the retribution which would follow once they had him behind closed doors, had his stomach in knots. His empty stomach, which in spite of his real and imagined terrors, called for breakfast. He would feel better after a strong cup of tea and a couple of fried eggs.

Look on the bright side, he told himself. He would sort things out. He always had before. Things would not look half so dark with some food inside him. Still he kept his wits about him, and his eyes open, as he made his way to Ma Weston's little café behind the nappy factory.

"One last deal," he told himself as he crossed the road. "One more scam, just one, a good 'un," he repeated as he cut through Colliers Alley.

"One last score and off to somewhere quiet and warm." He couldn't face another winter like the last.

Just as he turned the corner into Bullion Street some instinct made him glance over his shoulder. There, not fifty yards away, waiting for a gap in the busy traffic were Dave and Donald...Death and Destruction, Lenny Hand's driver and gardener.
Some gardener; more adept at pulling out fingernails than pulling out nettles.

Had they seen him though? He thought that they had, although he was by no means certain. Breakfast would have to wait.

Into Woolworths he went and out the side entrance, under the railway arch, up Pen Street and across to the Golden Lion. Down the little alleyway which ran along the side into Marsh Road. Was that Lenny's old Jag?

Struth, he was getting too old for all this ducking and diving. His breath was coming in short heavy bursts now, but there appeared to be little oxygen in the air and his legs began to feel like jelly. Twice he nearly slipped, and once he almost fell and would have done too if there had not been a parking meter handy. He regained his balance just in time to save himself. Thus distracted, he failed to notice that his nearly empty wallet had bounced out of his jacket pocket and fell silently upon the pavement where Marsh Road changes its name, becomes Fore Street and changes to cobbles as it joins the road which drops down into Market Square.

He had not noticed its loss, but Max Segal had seen it, and picked it up quickly. "Oi Mister – stop!" he yelled as he ran to return the wallet to its rightful owner. Its rightful owner was in no frame of mind to stop even for a second and adrenaline-funded energy, born out of terror, flowed into his lower limbs.

His heart was pounding like a steam engine now and he recognised the black fringe on the periphery of his vision which foretold of imminent unconsciousness. He must stop for a moment, take stock, and sit down, or nature and old age would do for him what Lenny's boys would do if they found him. Mother Nature might very well save them the trouble.

On his right hand side he suddenly noticed a blue door set in a long grey wall, which was half ajar. He burst through, closing it behind him, and tried to look as if he had business there. What was this place with its neat lawns and pretty flower beds? Oh yes, he knew well enough, this was the back of Eggbert House, part hospital, part old peoples rest home and part loonie bin.

About half were private patients, and half were people locked up for their own good by caring relatives who couldn't bear to have them at home drinking all the booze, and teaching the children how to swear. The staff were mostly Poles or Philippinos, caring people in their own way I suppose, but when they picked up enough English to get by they hopped it a bit smartish to find cleaner and better compensated employment elsewhere.

Staff turnover was rather high; shifts and rotas changed without notice and sometimes the residents wandered off into the grounds or into the town. Occasionally the were lost for several days at a stretch, but they always came back, sooner or later. Nobody on the staff made much of an effort to round up the lost sheep, but they dutifully phoned the police, rang the bell in the clock tower and sent a pager message to the orderlies to keep a watch out.

Seeing the wallet all but empty Max Segal pocketed a book of stamps and threw it into the bushes where moments later it was picked up by a monkey faced old man in a grubby Vicuna overcoat several sizes too large. Of the items overlooked or discounted by Max Segal was a return half of a ticket to Pinner and an envelope giving an address in Waxwell Lane. Thus equipped he proceeded to make his way there without further delay.

At the top of an ornate flight of stone steps Roger's heart, lungs, legs and sense of balance finally deserted him in protest and he fell, falling with all the grace and obedience to gravity of a sack of old boots. With a dull thud, his head connected with the York stone paving, tearing the skin, raising an instant bruise and knocking out two cosmetically enhanced teeth. He came round quite quickly, all things considered ,to find himself in the arms of a female orderly and a black doctor gently putting sutures in his head.

'Lie easy good sir and you will be as right as nine-pence. All hunky dory in just two ticks. Follow my finger if you can. Good. That is just fine. All is fine, no internal damage. Tell me, good sir, who is the prime minister?"

For all his recent trauma Roger rose to the challenge.

"My prime minister or yours?" he said, although he could not have named a single African prime minister.

However, although that was what he said, the sound which fell out of his bruised mouth with its burden of broken teeth and clotting blood was, "Mu propmisker er jaws?"

"Aha," said Dr N'Bobulus, "concussion I see." And your name, sir, if I might make so bold?"

Roger swallowed hard and said, "Woger Alaanwoo."

"Good, good we make progress. I do believe we have found our runaway. Okay old fellow, you just lay still. You, orderly, would you find a wheelchair and take Mr Alenby back to his ward. If you would be so kind."

Walking from Pinner Underground Station the monkey-faced man, Roger Alenby, walked past a dark Ford van parked close to the gate of The Elm's, Waxwell Lane. He sauntered up the path and stopped at the front door wondering what he was doing here. He thought that he was going home to Doris, but he didn't recognise this place at all. Where was Doris? Why didn't she answer the door? He wanted his tea. Whatever else he wanted we shall never know, for Donald's blackjack caught him with great precision in exactly the right spot behind his left ear. If the blanket thrown over his head and the duct tape over his mouth had not killed him, the shock, ten hours later of his sudden immersion in the deep cold waters of Rickswell Quarry would have. But just to be on the safe side, the Death and Destruction boys had tied his legs to a moped before heaving him in with a most satisfactory splash. Lenny would be pleased.

Roger Allenwood fought his way through a sedative fog to consciousness, and as sensation came back into his battered face, he concluded that he had been worked over. But no, and piece by piece it all came flooding back to him. He cautiously opened an eye. A group of about half a dozen stood around his bed grinning like tormented lizards. "Whoop, whoop," said one.

"Pollyfiller for tea. Pollyfiller for lunch. Pollyfiller for president," said another. "Whoop whoop."

"Excuse me friend, you've been there, yes. Was Leon Trotsky there?"

"Whoop, whoop."

Good God what was this place? If he had any doubt that he had fallen, quite literally into the company of nutters, the doubts did not linger long. He had to get out of here and pronto. Seeing him fully awake provided the signal they all wanted. They pressed closer.

The porcine Chinaman with the tattoo of a spider on his nose continued to whoop in welcome. Whoop, Whoop, Whoop.

One began to click his teeth click, click – pause - click click. The cries and shouts had, I suspect, on other occasions provided a ready catalyst to those new arrivals who, whilst not totally round the twist, found the conversion both simple and highly recommended both by words and example. The Lord is coming. Praise the Lord in Halifax unto the end of the earth. Oh the blood of the lamb. Jesus bids us eat but not without mint sauce. Click click. Whoop whoop. Pollyfiller Jesus the lamb."

"Here she comes." Screamed a youth, "The nym nym aa showers. Titties, s-showers, s -sch. Touching, touching my p' p' pa."

"Thank you, Peter, for looking after Mr Alenby. How are you this morning Roger after all that excitement yesterday?"

Her accent was Polish for sure, but her English was excellent.

"How are your teeth? Our doctor had to take them out I am afraid. Do you think that you can handle a soft boiled egg? Breakfast, then a bath. Yes?"

On the other side of the ward Peter started up like a lawnmower" Na Na Na P P P Pur."

Roger was about to tell her that it was all a monstrous mistake; that he didn't belong here and that his name was Allenwood not Alenby, when he caught a glimpse of the headline of the newspaper balanced on the adjacent bed. It read "The body of Roger Allenwood, Chief Executive Officer of K.I.P. investments was recovered earlier today from a disused Quarry in Rickswell. A dark blue Ford van was seen driving away by birdwatcher Pat Harris who witnessed the whole incident. Police are appealing for other witnesses to come forward.

"Good God, I'm reading my own obituary," he said.

The breakfast being served to the other residents looked and smelt delicious. He had been in and out of consciousness for two days, and had eaten little the day before that. So with the smell of bacon in his nostrils, he gulped down his soft boiled egg with relish, and thought about lunch. He picked up the newspaper. Well, that was that. Lenny Hand wouldn't be looking for him any more. He had a breathing space at last. In fact, Lenny identified the body, which is playing fast and loose with the legal system if you like. Lenny only met him the once so the body must have passed muster.

"We were like brothers," he is reported to have said. "I will miss him enormously."

"Yes," he thought. "Every time he thinks of the thirty grand he will never see again."

P P P Peter was right about one thing. Ward orderly Maria did take liberties with one's person at bath time. Not that he was one to complain on that account.

Outside the long summer ended abruptly and the wind threw handfuls of hailstones at the windows. He shivered. It was warm in here. Not every one of the inmates were crazy, some were quite sharp and good company, just frail, old and unloved. The food was excellent and plentiful, if basic, and the accommodation was free. He was counting his blessings. Bath time was more fun than he could remember. Lenny and his bums thought him dead, as did the bank of course.

He would, he decided, over winter here, build up his reserves, get a set of dentures and grow a beard. He must work out a way of showing steady progress in his mental state and if he could quietly investigate the position of Roger Alenby's estate, there might be money there if he could get his hands on it by proving himself sane. Bit risky of course, but if it didn't work out then next May or June he would slip quietly away.

He had to balance the risks. On the one hand here was a free billet safe and warm, with a bit of hanky-panky thrown in for good measure. Outside one of Lenny Hand's mob might recognise him, or - as was more likely - some other villain might get hold of the full S P and would want to rub Lenny's nose right in it, just for laughs. Then, for all he knew the real Roger Alenby might still be out there and up to something on his own account.

The bank would want to talk to him if they knew he was still alive. Not to mention the police who might be thinking in terms of fraud, identity theft and the death of the poor sod they had pulled out of the drink. God knows why they had assumed that it was him, but they would be sure to think that he had something to do with the murder when they realised that it wasn't his body. Then there was the Inland Revenue, the National Insurance people, and – hell's teeth – the VAT bloodhounds.

They never give up. They would follow Ulysses into Hades if they thought they could get their percentage out. About the only people he was good with was the Child Support Agency, at least he thought so, well pretty much, he hoped. But hold on. What if he really could squeeze some cash out of the Alenby estate? He might be able to set up an operation like this one. Rich old villains only of course. Get them to give him power of attorney over their finances, just a little bit of blackmail to change their will in his favour. Oh yes. He could see it all now, could picture it. The very thought of having a bunch of crooks like a geriatric Lenny Hand completely in his power..

Now that would be sailing very close to the wind indeed.

# A TIME TO LIVE AND A TIME TO DIE

The cover on my sleeping tube slid back with Germanic precision, accompanied by a soft hiss from the pneumatic actuators while a polished female voice called me to consciousness. It was a voice artfully created to awaken, but not arouse a man at the end of a sixty year journey at half the speed of light; our lives entrusted to a Japanese autopilot and guardian that never paused to sleep. The electrodes attached to my skull fell away as I blinked at the unaccustomed light, my mouth too dry to spit, felt parched and metallic in spite of having been automatically irrigated from time to time. I had anticipated that my first waking thoughts would have been of Laura, but all I could think of was a steaming mug of tea.

"Come over here Guns, this'll wake you up." I half-walked and half-floated over to the captain's command station.

On the Visual Display Unit a planet filled the screen. I caught my breath, "Wow".

An incredibly blue aqueous planet revolved slowly beneath us. Wreathed in drifting snowy white clouds it was beautiful from icy pole to icy pole. Fresh and clean as had been the Earth of my childhood before we … before we … No, it's still too painful to remember and yet here was a new chance to start over, to learn from the terrible mistakes we had made; mistakes we continued to make even when we knew better. All our hopes resided in this new home, the five hundred colonists in deep sleep in the hold and our small crew.

The skipper was a man of above average empathy and let me revel in the unrepeatable wonderment. Words have their uses and their limitations. I am only a simple soldier and words failed me. To say it was a sapphire on a bed of black velvet would be to denigrate the vista before me. It's foolish I know, but I seemed to hear its sonorous basso profundo notes calling to us in ease and quietude as it majestically turned before me. Clouds formed up over the oceans and fell as rain over the land to swell its long broad rivers. After long minutes I turned to the captain, "Any sign of life Skipper?"

"Lots, but only the middle continent is inhabited. Boats of course, but only small coasters. Nothing up to an ocean crossing. Some aircraft too, small, short duration jobs, fighters. I'll show you but first look at this."

The technicians had laboriously unpacked the big telescope and pointed it towards the larger continent and its western seaboard. It looked so peaceful; farms surrounded by patchwork fields, rivers and streams, woods, roads, towns and villages. Watermills and factories whose tall chimneys belched white and grey smoke high in the temperate air. It was all so normal that a more nostalgic man than I might have wept at such a welcoming new home. From the way the trees were turning I guessed that it must be autumn in the northern hemisphere and wondered what winter might be like.

"Now Guns, have a look at this. This it'll knock your socks off."

The big scope refocused on to the centre of this pastoral continent to where a hot, dirty war was blazing. Big guns, trenches, barbed wire, mud and shell holes. The full works.

From the great lakes in the south to the mountains in the north, young men fought and died over a front of 2000 miles or more; a long thin grey obscene gash, while less than fifty miles behind the lines, apples were being harvested by pretty girls in red and blue summer frocks not knowing if their loved ones were alive or dead. It was madness.

The dispute, whatever it's cause looked insane from where we were.

"Just like Earth Skipper," I said, sounding trite but not meaning to. We had both lost friends to war.

"Just like Earth, but it's not Earth, Major Wilson," he said sharply. It was the first time in ages he had called me anything except Guns. It was clear even to my dull insensitive mind that he would be feeling for those men down there whose bodies were being ripped apart and their minds shattered.

"So, Guns, what are we going to do about all this?" he said with a wave of the hand across the big screen.

"They'll not thank us if we interfere; take sides Skipper. Best let them work out their own destiny. Let them get on with it. It's no business of ours, cruel as that might sound. It might be more in keeping with our mission to land our cargo of colonists on one of the other continents. Find a nice sheltered spot, not too far north or south, Flattish agricultural land near a lake or a river and ..."

The skipper grunted at my cynicism, not realising for once that I had had my fill of conflict back on Earth as I watched, and at times, took part in its self destruction. Our world, my world, tore itself to shreds in fights for water, minerals, energy and finally, air to breathe.

'Ha'm, yes Guns … I can see your point and no doubt if we were to put it to the vote that would be the outcome. The thing is, Guns, if we did as you propose it would be a couple of generations at least to even begin to build the infrastructure we would need to make life tolerably comfortable. And who can say that the new generations might choose to live as savages or nomads. Tribal gangs ruled by bloody warlords. Are you prepared to gamble with the entire world's heritage? We have enough with us to get things off to a flying start but we need to plant what remains of our culture in fertile soil. I can't bear the thought that no-one would ever hear a full orchestra ever again, or read a poem out loud, or write a book. Can you?"

He was right of course, and I wondered if I looked as foolish as I felt.

'As I see it, Guns, we can't go back to Earth whatever we decide to do. We don't know enough to take sides in this bloody war even though with our weaponry we could crush one side or another in an afternoon. It's a pretty poor way to start a new life. So for now we must simply watch and wait, and learn all we can.

For two weeks that's exactly what we did, the hours hanging like never ripening fruit before the minds eye. A multiplicity of idle lusts and fancies bloomed and fell like petals at my feet, sleep and dreams the only respite from the monotony.

By the tenth day I would have forsaken all the women in creation for a long walk beneath those bronzed autumnal trees, breathing in great lungfuls of country air scented with the tang of wood smoke.

The air in the ship filtered, cleaned and recycled a million times still smelled of plastic and hot circuitry. Stale air, synthetic food and processed water. I was sick of it and began to wander between decks at all hours for no purpose; just to kill time. Seeing my agitation, the captain sent me on a mission to investigate the arms industry down there. It was my speciality after all; it was one of the reasons I was here.

Dressed in what I hoped would be a fair facsimile of a wounded officer's uniform the helipod landed me just before local dawn on the outskirts of a large city, and some twenty miles distant. Further than I would have wished, but the most secure option. It was rather colder than I had anticipated too, and an early frost crunched and crackled underfoot. I walked through sleepy villages of white shabby cottages, my footsteps echoing down the near empty streets, with each passing mile the thought growing and developing - yes, I could live here. A little farm or a factory perhaps, even a pub. Did they have pubs here? I hadn't seen any.

It was so exciting just to be there. A spy on a strange world. A stranger in a strange land. A stranger stranger than its inhabitants could ever imagine. What do they do to spies here? Shoot them or something more horrible? Pushing these and other random fears aside was easy. I felt so at home here.

It was all so familiar, like Kent or Devon perhaps. It was like England but it wasn't. I must be guarded. Still the brambles, stone walls, and five bar gates could have been anywhere. Whole streets seemed to remind me of, no, not reminded - wrong word. The houses evoked in me a feeling of London's 19th Century suburbs: Norwood, Highgate, Dulwich or Islington perhaps. Solid grey brick Victorian structures with high gables, peeling paintwork and neglected gardens; gardens which once must have been very grand indeed.

Were it not for the strange looking cars, few and far between, or the occasional military truck one could easily be fooled into believing that this was Earth, and that our ship had somehow twisted time and space in some unfathomable way.

The few people that were out and about were women, some like grey scurrying mice. Others bowed, black bereaved beetles, alone and adrift upon the ocean of recent grief which lay spread before them in their remaining years.

Here and there a flash of colour which came and went like the merest zephyr of femininity in this strange place. One looked just like my sister. Another, like the girl in the grocers on Hill Street and another like ..........

I pulled myself up short. This was foolish, dangerous even, this seeing familiarity in everything. I had a job to do. I walked on quickly but the disturbing associations had not done with me yet. Not by a long chalk. I turned a corner and there before me a scene right out of a Grimshaw painting; one of those inspired by his visit to Hampstead in the 1880s, where a sad beauty born of nostalgia was locked in time for ever. Red brick villas which glowed in the sunshine next to solid mercantile castles, whose grey masonry was once ebullient golden sandstone. It was all too much. Frozen fingers grabbed my insides with an impetus of fear, which might have been excitement had I not suspected the onset of madness. I began to tremble and felt the first pang of panic. I had to get a grip on all of this before blindly moving on and running into who knows what situation.

Then as welcome as it was sudden and unexpected, at the back of my boiling mind, beyond the wonder, excitement, and terror, another voice, very small and calm. "This was home, everything would work out fine, have faith," and if I should die here, well that would be okay too.

It was as if something about this place knew what I knew, or guessed or surmised. Some mechanism set up to play games with my mind, taunting me with hints and suggestions of things past. A sort of process of projection, an illusion working itself out as though in a dream. Every subjective experience I had had since my arrival was like something, but not something. Intimations of unreality pressed in upon me until the world span and I feared that I might pass out. I leaned upon a tall wrought iron gate in front of a grand house to collect my thoughts. It was black and solid, cold and very real. For once in my life reason did not come to my assistance and dark thoughts fluttered through my mind like bats.

A woman opened the door of the house and tripped swiftly down the long pathway to the gate. I was, after all, wearing the uniform of a recuperating officer. This was the first woman in this place I had seen up close. Not beautiful some might say. Small and thin with large dark eyes. Delicate hands with short fingernails. Lips made for smiling, but clearly had had nothing to smile about in a long time.

She spoke, and there it was again, that feeling of something half-remembered, half-known, half-revealed.

It was an English voice, but it was not English which she spoke. Somehow it was like English and sooner than I would have thought possible I could understand. Not a whole lot you understand, but I caught first her name, Phaedra, and then the meaning of her questions. Don't ask me how, I can't even offer a speculative answer.

At first she wanted news of the war. I shook my head as if it were all too painful to discuss. In reality I knew nothing about it. Her eyes would dart from time to time to a photo in a tarnished frame. An officer, wearing the wings of an airman upon his tunic. I thought that he looked a lot like me, but younger. As far as I knew there was not a woman anywhere who would put my photo in a frame, silver or otherwise.

This was a woman a man might live for and, curse me for a romantic fool, a woman a man might die for. It was her voice more than anything that would snare a man's soul and take it from him; a voice which epitomised, like nothing else, the mystical, resigned, melancholic, poetic, shawl which time and suffering had wrapped around her. Not a woman made for love, but made of love. I knew then that I loved her. All my thoughts and feelings came together in a split second at that point. in the realisation that some power to some purpose had brought us together here far away from the place of my birth across the immeasurable gulf that separated her world from mine.

All thoughts of my ship, my mission and my companions were relegated to the wings as mere props and supporting cast in this very real drama. All too aware that I could never return home. I had but one objective; which was to live and die here with this delightful creature. If only - ah, if *only* - she would allow me to replace in her affection the husband or lover in the blackened silver frame.

She sat me in an armchair by the window while she went off to make tea. It was a room I might have decorated myself, a grander example of the flat I had left behind me on Earth. There were watercolours and mahogany furniture, delicate oil lamps and polished brass, walls lined with books bound in leather. I picked up a pipe and began to fill it absentmindedly from an ornate stone jar. I quickly put it aside as she entered the room with the tea things, lest she see my impertinence.

We sat for a while in silence sipping hot tea. It was like tea but it was not tea. Like the streets, like the houses, like the planet, it was like Earth, but it was not Earth. My questions hung in the air like the motes of dust caught in the last rays of the setting sun. It ought to have been unsettling; perhaps it was in a way, but I could not suppress a long suppressed germ of happiness, which was worming its way out, and there was not a thing I could do to understand

107

it, much less suppress it.

On the ornate carved over mantle an elaborate clock doled out the seconds with commendable economy. Leaves swirled on the veranda, and a lazy west wind spoke of a seductive ease. Without question this was where I belonged and would remain but ... the picture in the blackened silver frame seamed to grin. Did its tarnish signify that he was dead, this airman who looked so much like me? Did he care, did he give me his blessing? We might have been brothers. I pictured his fragile aircraft crashing in flames. I could see him scream, but could not hear. I too screamed inwardly at the thought of such a death consigned to the flames as he fell from the sky, knowing that he would never see his girl again.

I shivered at a sudden draught. The house was full of draughts. The heavy brocade curtains did move just a little then. She noticed my shiver, for her eyes had scarcely left me. With a tilt of the head she bid me light the fire which lay ready, awaiting just a match. It was well laid with newspaper, twigs and coal. A servant laid this, I thought. It caught swiftly and soon little dragons of flame and sulphurous fumes erupted from pockets of gas trapped within the coal. A little smoke drifted into the room, but not much. I turned with a childish pride in my small achievement and was rewarded with a smile. The sun had almost set now behind the tall elm trees over yonder, draining their leaves of colour and casting the parlour into shadow.

How soft and how sad her features in the flickering firelight. And again vehement, insistent, all persuasive, the same thought - that we belonged together in an eternal future of our own making. The die was cast, for ever and beyond, in and out of all the skeins of twisted and incomprehensible time and distance. Together, beyond life beyond death, and beyond the universe, through the conspiracy of a trillion parallel universes to make a happy reality of two insignificant scraps of existence. Mere punctuation marks between the never was and the ever was.

More smoke was blowing back into the room now, filling every nook and cranny with its foul yellow choking reek. Phaedra. I called out her name in panic. I called again and again, blood pounding in my ears, but each and every breath caused me to choke and gasp for air, lungs screaming, I fell to my knees and the world began to spin.

Death would be tolerable if she were there and let me hold her hand and hear her voice one more time. For a moment there was silence, the silence of the grave, Then voices, other harder masculine voices. Voices I half-recognised, voices edged with panic, growing louder.

"Damn you Sparks, just do it."

"But if I do it, Skipper, the colonists in the hold will suffocate and die. Is that what you want?"

"And if we all die first? Is that what you want?"

"Please buy me some time, Sparks, I need some time to think. Clear this mess, use their air to do it."

Huge fans sucked out the smoke from the control cabin replacing it with clean air from the hold. Smoke still seeped in from conduits and minor ducts.

"Whats happening, Skipper?"

The Skipper turned towards me, his hair gone and his face lined and wrinkled. There were tears in his yellow bloodshot eyes.

"Ah, Guns, you're awake at last. Thing is, Guns, we never left Earth orbit. Some technical cock up. We have been in Earth orbit for 60 years. We were supposed to be frozen, suspended, but that went wrong too. We just got older and older. Most of the crew died years ago, most of the colonists too, I shouldn't wonder. We would have slept for ever but for a piece of rock or space debris. Some bloody thing sheared off our starboard sponson, taking our fuel and life support system with it. The alarm system woke us up. Looks like this is the end, Guns."

He held out his hand and I noticed that my fingers, like his, were mere yellowing sticks which ached as we shook hands for the last time.

Returning to my transit sleeping tube I closed the cover and turned on the small reserve flask of oxygen as the world of the control deck filled once again with smoke and the lights dimmed before going out completely.

I awoke between crisp linen sheets, scented with lavender. An early autumn sunrise lit up the rose patterned wallpaper, and the blue and white jug on the washstand. Outside wood pigeons cooed, and in the distance a truck rumbled along an unmade road.

Beside me in the crook of my arm asleep, breathing softly, Phaedra. Small, neat and naked, her raven blue black hair spread out over the pillow.

How right it was to be here with this girl who had changed my life forever. The voices deep within me had spoken truly. I was indeed destined to stay here until the day I died.

# ONE LAST TRIP

Me'i Gui, known to her few English friends as May, bent with a twinge of pain to pick up her post from the mat and thought, somewhat ironically, that she might be pregnant, even though she knew that to be impossible.

Ever since her mother had died she had hated receiving the post in the morning. Bill, bill, circular, bill.

A small letter, whose importance - in her eyes - dwarfed the others and sat in her hand with a foreboding presence, which was far larger than the mere brown manila envelope which constrained it, bearing the franking mark of St Mary's.

With trembling fingers she slit it open and unfolded a singular sheet of white paper. It was indeed bad news, but to be fair no more so than the doctors had told her that she might expect. She had left it too late for the long treatment that would have been necessary to be of any practical use. It was also something which they would have wished to explain to her in person. But what with targets demanding their attention, staff shortages, form filling and the spending cuts that was not possible.

You know how it is. The much loved NHS had been living on a financial knife edge for years. The letter was polite, but formal. The results, although anticipated, struck her small frame like a punch. She had to sit down to weep long restrained silent tears.

I will not distress you with the full and unnecessary details of her condition, and of the consultant's prognosis except to say that she might expect six months to live as things were, with perhaps a further three or four on incremental doses of palliative medication.

There would come a time when no amount of pain killers would hold back the pain and her last days would not be pleasant. Ah, pain, that villainous old acquaintance that had followed her on and off all her life, through illness, broken bones and heartache.

It was a relentless and lascivious hound that would not stop until her bones were deep in the earth and beyond the reach of its insatiable jaws. Now it was so close she could feel its presence, hear it padding up behind her seeking revenge for all those aspirins, potions and balms which had kept it at bay all these long years.

Drying her tears upon a piece of kitchen roll she breathed deeply and whilst it would be true to say that she accepted her destiny with true oriental fatalistic dignity, there was something else too in the long profound sigh that it took her by surprise for a moment. It was an emotion which she neither expected nor understood. It was the feeling of relief. Relief that the worst was now over and that a limit had been set upon her torment. There was, she felt, something in this feeling that was cathartic, redemptive and calm.

Though these would not have been the words she would have chosen these were undoubtedly her feelings. In addition there was, behind this whirlpool of new feelings a resolution which grew moment by moment into a steel resolve to extract every last drip of excitement and pleasure from her remaining days.

That night she laid her comprehensive plans and sleep, when it came, was deep and sweet. Her dreams were dreams of paths untrod and wines untasted. And in those dreams vivid and full of colour there was music and a soft quiet voice which seemed to say in Chinese "Don't worry. Don't worry. Everything is going to be alright."

The following morning she dressed as though for a business meeting in a dress of Royal blue silk in the style known as a cheongsam, with a revealing slit which gave tantalising glimpses of her shapely legs as she walked, or settled into the rear seat of the black taxi which took her into town. Expensive, but what the dickens, you only live once, right. She liked the atmosphere in the office of UTIMATE EXPERIENCES INC. It was new, but strangely old-fashioned with its solid desks, heavy curtains and deep leather armchairs. The voyages, which were all expensive, offered almost everything for every taste. Cruises along the Nile, treks over the prairies in a Conestoga wagon, and the chance to see the Taj Mahal by moonlight from an old biplane. Now that would be something I might choose for myself one day. Who knows?

For M'ei Gui there was no dilemma, it just had to be a cruise. If she closed her eyes she was there already; the luxury first class cabin, silk sheets and ice cold champagne. Lots and lots of champagne, and there would be peaches too; the paddle steamer plashing its way across the broad blue Pacific.

Dinner at the Captain's table, waltzing with the handsome first officer, to the music of a full band. It was a scenario she pictured a hundred times before the scheduled day finally arrived. At the front door she turned to look one last time at her little cosy home, with its freshly watered plants and the handful of heavy serious letters propped conveniently in the toast rack on the dining room table, and without another thought she was off at last on the greatest adventure of her life.

A cheerful cockney seaman carried her bags aboard, and a junior officer introduced her to her stateroom, all polished brass and mahogany. There were deck games, a quartet on the quarterdeck, cocktails and parties, a fancy dress ball and a boisterous crossing-the-equator ceremony. The sun blazed down from a baby blue sky and even thoughts of her illness could not cast a cloud upon the horizon of her happiness. They rounded Cape Horn in an exciting storm, which was but a mere taste of the hurricane which was to follow as the bow of their brave little ship bit into the long Pacific rollers. This too was exciting, more than exciting, it was frightening. A rogue wave hit the ship broadside on and sent glasses and cutlery spinning.

"We apologise for any inconvenience," said the Captain over the tannoy in a calm, well modulated English voice. "The radio tells us we are in for a bit of a blow," which for the initiated was code for there was even worse dirty weather ahead.

"Nothing to worry about, we'll alter course in a bit and ought to avoid the worst of it. Still it might get a little rough. So just to be on the safe side the open deck areas will be off limits for passengers and crew until it blows over. All on duty seamen to storm stations please, and would all passengers see that all their breakables are safely stowed away in their cabins. Thank you."

M'ei Gui wasn't about to miss a thing, and found a stout comfortable chair in the middle of the first class observation deck with its vast reinforced plate glass windows.

The sun sets very quickly in the tropics and it was soon pitch black. Very occasionally a worried moon would peek through ragged racing clouds to reveal a purple oily ocean, upon which their little steamer bobbed and pitched as though it were doing something for a dare. Great white capped waves streamed along the pitching deck hurling spray high into the air at each obstruction before the howling wind swept it away and threw it like angry gravel at the window where she sat enthralled.

A kindly old gentleman with grey hair placed a strong steadying arm gently around her shoulders and reassured her that all would be well. He had been a soldier and had sailed through hundreds of these tropical storms. As if to refute his comforting remarks, and at the same time call him a fool to belittle the power of the sea, a bolt of lightening split the heavens. The peal of thunder hard upon its heels could be felt as well as heard.

With stoic abandon, and it had little choice to be other, the steamer pushed onward into the petulant angry storm. Crash followed flash again and again. The first class passengers were split about 50-50 between the genuinely petrified and the elated. Flash-boom. Flash-boom. The thunder and the lightening were almost continuous at times. More than one would have remembered friends lost in recent wars to bomb and shell, but the unspoken conspiracy of survivors held, and no-one spoke of such terrible things.

The rain was falling like silver steel wires against the blackness, washing the encrusted salt from the plate glass and … What was that? There look – just... Can't you see it man? For God's sake look. There. Yes there.

It's another ship, having a hard time too by the look of it. I wonder if the Captain's spotted it. It's got its lights out and oh God it's almost broadside on to the waves. Surely it must flounder and sink?

The Captain had seen it of course. He was a professional master and he swiftly ordered a 4 degree turn to port. There could be no harsh manoeuvring in this filth.

It was then, as her head settled upon her new course, that the bolts securing her transmission cross-head sheared, and the great paddle wheels came to an abrupt halt, the helm lifeless in the cox'ns hands. Without power she was dead in the water, helpless, unable to manoeuvre or make headway. The storm had her now like a little rat in the jaws of a big dog.

As if drawn by a strange herding instinct the two ships began to close, drawing ever closer together. Upon closer examination the second ship was not a ship at all, but a part of one. A fraction of its former self, a prior disaster had ripped away its stern and most of its mid section. The bows of this nameless hulk, with all the malevolence of a battleaxe carried by the strong unfeeling wind and encouraged in its endeavour by uncaring waves, bore down upon its quarry.

The paddle steamer's searchlight picked her out in its icy beam and greeted her for what she was; a cruel harbinger of death. Sinister and red with rust. She had been at sea for what? Thirty years? Fifty then. A very long time indeed. Soon she would be free from her curse and need wander no more. For soon she would sleep at rest in the deep, together with so many who'd had cause to hazard upon this ocean in the pursuit of pleasure, gain or destiny.

To M'ei Gui and the other awe-stricken passengers, how quickly the gap closed between the two vessels. Suddenly there it was huge and jealous of life. Its bow rose up and like a desperate, hungry, living thing, bit down hard into the side of the little steamer. "If I must die we must both die."

Within hurried, but practiced seconds - or so it seemed to her - she and a dozen others were safely seated in Number One Lifeboat. Did I say safely? I did didn't I? I spoke too soon, for a buoyant piece of flotsam, an oil tank or cistern, appeared bobbing excitedly beside them until - like a hideous brown pugilistic fist - it chanced to strike their frail lifeboat pinning it to the sinking steamer. Smashing timbers and tearing limbs, tossing the silent dead, and screaming, praying living into the churning sea.

This was not the surprise she had anticipated when she had paid over her money, signed a contract and purchased her ticket from ULTIMATE EXPERENCES INC back in London.

As dark and as long as the storm of the night was in its fear and despair, so the dawn came with its becalmed sea, light and warmth. She could, and did, weep with joy when she saw, a short way off, say fifty yards or so, the white sand and waving palms of a coral island. She tried to swim, but she was too exhausted. Still the waves in guilty compensation carried her gently onward until her bare feet touched the warm welcoming sand.

Her shoes had gone and her lovely white dress was in rags, but she was safe and she was not alone, for to her left a girl was walking towards her. It was … but no. She had forgotten her name, but a teenager about her age from the second class deck.

All she wore was a strip of torn cloth about her hips and seemed quite in her element here on this little island miles from anywhere.

"Hello – it's May isn't it? I am Diana," she said softly, reaching out to touch M'ei Gui's cheek as if testing reality.

"It was a horrible storm wasn't it?"

"Yes," said M'ei Gui, so happy to have found a friend who had survived the events of the night.

"Are you hungry? I am. Let's explore."

"M'ei Gui, still unsteady, followed her new friend watching and wondering where she was and where they were heading. With slow exhausted footsteps she dawdled, but followed anyway as the sun rose, and the day became hot with the mist rising from the trees inland.

Diana, in response to some secret amusing thought, splashed around in the surf laughing as M'ei Gui clutched her ragged dress about her as if it were all that separated her from savagery.

Then as they crossed a sandy spit they saw, or rather smelt, wood smoke, and there it was - in a small clearing a crackling fire in a hearth of stones upon which sizzled small silver fish, and from the nearby trees the thwack of an axe or machette. Diana recognised the axeman at once "It's Henry, darling Henry." Dear sweet Henry, to whom she had been so off-hand and dismissive on board ship. Henry, Second Engineer, turned open-mouthed as he saw these two girls walking towards him, one half-naked, the other in the tattered remains of a Bond Street dress.

"Well, what shall we do now?" asked Diana when they had eaten the tiny fishes, and shared a huge crab roasted in the embers of the fire with sweet bananas.

"Over there," said Henry pointing with a stick. "I think I saw a house of sorts. Can't be sure of course. I lost my glasses when the boat sank, but if it *is* one and we stay together, we can get there before dark."

The remains of their meal remained where they fell as they walked from the soft sand of the beach and cautiously picked their way through the rocks and up onto the ridge of a hill. It was a house to be sure, a white bungalow with a water tank on stilts and a wind-driven pump or generator on a hill beyond. Like Livingstone, Henry slashed a way through the undergrowth until they crossed a narrow pathway. After that it was easy going and they made good progress.

Parakeets screeched, finches twittered and a million butterflies rose up to greet them in a great psychedelic welcome. As M'ei Gui followed behind Diana watching her fair hair bobbing about her bare shoulders she felt too that this was nothing more than a strange and wonderful dream. If it was a dream what did anything matter if ...? Her conscious mind caught the beautiful, but unwelcome thought, like a steel trap, and she put it from her mind.

Abruptly they came to the bungalow; bigger than they had thought, but unlocked and deserted. It had a pool in the yard and a spa bath on the veranda, electric lights that refused to work and a larder full of tinned goods. There were books and music, oriental rugs upon the bare boards, and a sensuous but not indelicate painting above the fireplace. Diana made a new sarong from a bright towel and M'ei Gui improvised a dress from an artfully folded lace curtain tied together with a silken curtain cord, so that when she looked at herself in the mirror she felt quite civilised. From the corner of her eye she saw Diana fixing her hair, looking every inch a tease and a savage, her fingers fluttering over her bare breasts and her blue-grey eyes sparkling with mischief.

With her long freshly brushed hair in a ponytail, M'ei Gui joined Henry in the garden picking mangoes, bananas, oranges, papayas and bread fruit. They worked well together but in silence. If Henry had given any thought to being shipwrecked on a desert island with two beautiful girls, he did not say. His feelings, however, were easier to imagine.

When they returned, Diana ran to greet them, skipping up and down like a child eager to please, and immensely proud of the table she had laid. Tonight they would dine on china plates with silver cutlery, beneath the soft light of beeswax candles. There were even finger bowls and table napkins. These things were all set out together with polished glasses upon an old - but splendid - damask tablecloth. The effect was rich but simple. The owner must be a person of consequence for simplicity of this sort was always expensive. In a rocky basement they found an armoury and an extensive wine cellar. Henry, who liked to believe that he had a fine taste in such things pulled out two bottles of Krug and a splendid old port covered in cobwebs, and a bottle of brandy. The sun was just about set to disappear in its watery bed when they sat down to supper. Diana tore into both the fruit and the champagne with an impish excitement. The others were more careful, but perhaps not careful enough. But what is caution to a teenager when the evening breeze is stirring the oleander, orchids and ginger flowers, and the evening's intoxicating cocktail is one of relief, youth and exuberance? There was electricity in the air; something of a certain, or rather uncertain, tension to which they could not put a name. Only Diana seemed immune. Immune or beyond caring as she refilled her glass again and again.

Henry reached out a hand to steady her as she nearly upset the table. The fine blond hairs on his arm looked so downy and baby-like that M'ei Gui wanted to reach out and cover his large hand with her small one, as if to reassure him by saying, "I know, I know, calm yourself, for you will only be hurt by those devil may care eyes of hers. Those perfectly bronzed shoulders swept by that golden hair. Not to mention those magnificent breasts but it's not ..."

Not what? What was she thinking of and not saying? Try as she might she still could not sponge those thoughts; mad, tender and foolish thoughts which had oiled their way into her mind as she had walked along from the beach behind that strong young back and long legs. Even when she tore her glance away, there was Henry laying about him with a machete as though he were a pirate with a cutlass. Like spectators, they watched as Diana reached for the last slice of melon and watched as the juice ran down her chin dripping cool and sweet upon her breasts.

Henry's hand took on a life of its own and a forefinger gratuitously swept up a single drip which hung pearl-like from her breast, and lifting his finger to his lips inhaled as if by so doing he would draw the very soul of her into his own body. The second lasted an eternity and yet before she was even aware of the impulse M'ei Gui had done the same. Diana stood up tipsy and unsteady. Her chair fell over. What game was this? Did she ever need to ask? With one hand she drained her glass and with the other released the improvised sarong. She bit her knuckle to suppress an excited giggle, threw back her head, shook out her hair and said, "Well, here we all are."

M'ei Gui felt like an observer looking down from above upon her own life scarcely believing what she was doing stood beside her and pulled at the bow which secured her improvised curtain-dress. The lace fluttered to the floor. Henry silently thanked a god he had no belief in as he kicked his shorts aside. As if pre-arranged, in that moment the tropical sun set. The candles lit themselves as if by magic and a fire blazed up in its stainless steel hearth and roared into life as they came together in one huge embrace.

Fear and the nearness to death aboard the distressed steamer had lit a fuse which had been mouldering all day since they waded ashore. Now it was fizzing and sparkling, inching its way towards conflagration and explosion. Three tongues, six lips and thirty fingers sought out the hidden wells of their tenderness. This, all of this, was so very new to them. For when all was said and done they were still little more than children.

Above them and their mounting happiness a full moon veneered with gold and trimmed with silver clouds sailed magnificently over a purple ocean which teased the murmuring shifting sands running its fingers through a billion sea shells.

M'ei Gui, Diana and Henry were lost in one another now. For an hour or an eternity they clung together in a kaleidoscope of passion's bounty that knew neither boundary nor end. As she lay warm between them M'ei Gui realised that all her life had been but a test, and that in her heart of hearts she had lived for this experience and could die happily now with no regrets between these, her lovers. She could not remember pain neither could she recall or imagine a greater happiness. Outside the night echoed with the screech and howl of strange and unfamiliar nocturnal animals vocal in their pain or excitement.

The breeze in the dark leaved trees awoke the incessant chatter of the cicadas. It is all too easy, is it not, to imagine the cornucopia of feelings bound up in these entwined young bodies as they lay half awake and half asleep before the flickering orange firelight.

It is far too tempting to join them in imagination and too hard to hide our rough and ready feelings held hostage to the poverty of our own faltering steps on the pilgrimage that is love Jealousy or time-tinted nostalgia, it is no business of ours. For who knows wherefrom these young people had miraculously acquired such patience and tenderness, such sensuality and stamina for the clock moved with exquisitely sympathetic slowness. The stars crawled across the heavens, though between kisses and caresses the Earth itself stood still. Ultimately the celestial clockwork would not be denied and as the first rays of the sunlight marked the ceiling with prison bars of rose-coloured light, their love play reached its final climax. It is tempting to believe that for Henry the night they had spent together had opened a door upon a new and meaningful vision of the world and his understanding of love. For Diana it was perhaps the first link in a chain, which was to bind her to a life of sensations forever, be it a good or bad enslavement. For M'ei Gui it was her every wish, real, imagined, hoped for or simply wondered at.

She had cleansed and freed her soul. Even as the other two lay sweetly sleeping in each others arms, the warm sunlight on their naked bodies, little earthquakes and aftershocks racked M'ei Gui's tiny body. Her very blood was alive and on fire with rivers of pleasure until at last she too lay very still, at peace and blissfully happy.

In the back office at ULTIMATE EXPERIENCES INC there is a quiet and air conditioned control room and a duty officer who kept a watchful eye on their clients. Their clients had paid a fortune to join their programme. A whole life's savings in some cases. They had an obligation to monitor events. Dials, lights and computer screens are poor company at five in the morning. Laura Sexton looked up from her crossword in surprise as supervisor Alice Seagrave walked into the control room.

"Well, you look busy – what's on tonight?"

"Not much, Alice. Very quiet indeed. Only four running at the moment. Two Battle of Britain, that's 28 and 46. The last days of Robin Hood in 13 and a modified Blue Lagoon in cubicle number 33. Can't be much longer to run on that one. She came in early and the bio scan monitors have been all over the place."

"Please, Laura, I do wish you wouldn't call them cubicles, they are suites. Mr H insists upon a high professional standard right through the organisation,. not just the attractive boys and girls on the booking desk, but right across the operation. Even though it's been legal for twenty years, euthanasia is still a political hot potato. We have to be squeaky clean at every turn. Everything must be done by the book. What we do is important to lots of people, you do believe that don't you?"

A low pitched trill sounded as they both looked at the screen.

"That's the final infusion going into 'suite 33'. Not long now. It was but a few moments before a soft bell rang like a muted kitchen timer. As it sounded the central command screen lit up like a fruit machine with its chats and graphs.

"Wow," said Alice with a little whistle. "Will you look at that? Mr H will want to see this right away. Did you ever see such a high client satisfaction reading? Who is it?"

"No idea. She was in process when I came on shift. Paid cash in advance and had all the right paperwork by the look of it. Took the full works. Everything."

"That's unusual, not many pay up front. Make you wait for probate."

"If you want to stay here and keep an eye on the others, I'll go and help the exit team," she said, slipping a strong peppermint into her mouth and pulling on a pair of latex gloves. "Just another shift," she mused to herself as she was joined by her colleagues from legal and medical at the door of suite 33. "Shall we go in Doc?. Will you break the statutory seal and stop the clock or shall I?"

Inside the spherical cubicle, a tropical cinematic sea still broke gently upon a white sandy beach and gulls wheeled and cried overhead; lamenting, or so she thought, the passage of another soul upon its last journey. On the central bed festooned with wires and tubes and covered with sensory stimulation pads lay the small naked body of M'ei Gui, the tumour that would have killed her as large and obscene as a black grapefruit. A diabolic parody of a third breast.

Though not in their job description, they paused for a moment in unspoken prayer for the diminutive old lady who lay before them perfectly at ease and with such a pretty smile upon her wrinkled oriental face. The doctor took his readings and filled in his forms. The technician began to disconnect the hundreds of wires and dozens of tubes one after the other before dumping the sensory pads in a stainless steel container destined for incineration.

Alice had been in this class of work too long to be sentimental but even so, yes even so, she let out a huge breath and blew her nose upon a tissue. Ah well, one more satisfied customer of ULTIMATE EXPERIENCES INC.

# BLOODY HELL!

**T**ime was when all men and nearly all theologians believed in God, after their fashion, and could really tell good deeds from evil ones. Well, as they say, the road to hell is paved with good intentions.

We lived in a strange, un-natural and exciting world back then at the end of the last century. There was a kind of electrical excitement in the air, a palpable tension, generated by what you might call a social neurosis.

On the one hand there was the supercharged effervescent desire for change, improvement and novelty. On the other hand there was a heart felt craving, which welled up from deep within the archives of racial memory to go back across the deep chasm of time to an age of pastoral simplicity.

As it turned out, one man was able to deliver on both counts and died having made good on the second. Much to his dismay and chagrin I might add.

I knew him slightly you know. In my undergrad days at UCL. Different departments, though we were all in awe of his extroverted polymathematical showmanship, and the euphoric products of his unquestioned genius. The bulk of his studies centred upon the synthesis of protein. For being able to mass produce spiders silk, stronger than steel he received the Nobel Prize. For teaching us how to re-grow missing teeth from little seeds planted in the gums he received his knighthood.

But it was for the invention of U.P.B that he will be best remembered. Every child in every school learned of his name and his exploits, along with their times tables and elementary computer programming. Colleges, hospital wards and airports were named in his honour. There was even talk, for a time, in Papal circles that he was to be beatified. I can't confirm that of course but all things were possible before the church turned against him.

U.P.B. - Universal Plastic Blood - was as revolutionary in the medical world as Bessimer Steel had been in the world of engineering many years before. It was colourless, well almost, and

---

one grade suited everyone, animals included.

It readily accepted medications, but at the same time rejected germs, bacteria and virus infections. Leukaemia, AIDS and malaria vanished almost overnight and blood banks, like blood letting barber surgeons, became things of the Dark Ages.

The whole exchange procedure was simplicity itself; old blood out, new blood in and a quick burst of Gamma rays to set the process off.

One aspect of the new blood, and some would have said the greatest thing, was the way it carried and delivered oxygen. Nicotine, alcohol and heroin lost their power to enslave. Eyesight improved, and with extra oxygen in the system, sporting records were being broken every other day. Alan Rogers ran a mile in under three minutes. In fact, everyone who had the new blood installed was fundamentally changed. People were kinder, more generous, intelligent and aware. The new blood, being transparent, gave the body a magical luminous quality that is hard to describe; ethereal, some said, just like angels. A foretaste of heaven, one journalist said and I can't disagree, as the entire world over people discovered new perceptions and insights into the wonders of life. The chains of old illusions dropped away, scales fell from their eyes and, as you might imagine, the old prescriptive religions suffered in consequence. In fact they all but died out as far as the rank and file worshippers were concerned. Only the fanatics remained, kept their old blood and vociferously fumed at every opportunity. But even they could see by the evidence of their own eyes that the world had changed, and changed for the good. As the old rites and rituals fell away, newer, clearer and more honest institutions sprang up to take their place. It was the dawning of the Age of Aquarius.

Plastic Blood! Plastic People! I hear you scream. Was it not the tension, the angst, the obsessions, the neurosis and wild ambitions which made our world such an interesting and exciting place to live. Perhaps, yes, for some people at some times, but I for one breathed a deep sigh of relief when the world's atomic weapons were dumped on the far side of the moon, beyond use for all time.

You could spot the hard line religionists a mile off; their sluggish movements, anachronistic mode of dress, and dull skin. Not for them the Brave New World. At first it cost an absolute fortune to have the new blood installed, but as the wheels of industry turned it became almost free. Even third world dictators got in on the act and squirreled away the budget that would otherwise have been spent on hospitals. As you know, mosquitoes didn't care for it. Ticks, leeches and sharks even found it poisonous.

My one enduring memory of those days was the picture which still haunts my mind, asleep or awake, of Rebecca, Becky - my small delicate blonde girl. If I close my eyes even for a second there she is, her naked pearlescent skin lit up from within. God just had to exist to send me this three-dimensional angel to love. From the tips of her tiny toe nails to the top of her golden hair she was everything a man could wish for in a wife - smart and funny and kind. What a pair we made, everybody said so.

After much soul-searching, I was on the verge of having a blood exchange myself. My appointment was booked and a taxi arranged to take me to the clinic, but before I made the exchange she died.

One in a million chances they said. Extremely rare occurrence. Just a minor house fire at home. Cooking something nice for me I shouldn't wonder. The new oxygen-rich, hydrocarbon based blood burned furiously once started. Death would have been mercifully quick. I was devastated. My world simply fell apart and to this day I have never completely recovered. I couldn't hold down a job and, with the little money we had put by, moved to a run down cottage on the edge of Exmoor and stayed drunk for a decade, or so it seemed. All alone and shunned by the neighbours, which fortunately were few and far between, and endlessly playing snatches of Mahler on the violin. Writing my awful poetry and stewing in a cauldron of my own despond. As my consumption of whisky went up so my financial reserves went down, only my misery stayed on an even and unrelenting path.

Apart from its incendiary qualities, the new blood had one other fault. A fault so small, so infrequently encountered as to be no fault at all when offset against all the other benefits.

Under certain conditions, such as those found in a nuclear power station, some people - by no means all – but some unfortunate people would rapidly dehydrate with alarming suddenness. A scientist in California speculated that there was a correlation with sun spots or cosmic rays. We will never know for certain, and it is only of academic interest now anyway. When it was one in a billion it was just an interesting note in the margin, one in ten million was a curious phenomenon, but one in a million and The World Health Organisation sat up and began screaming for answers. Sales of U.P.B. slumped, but it was all too late.

On 1st April, April Fools Day, the world was given notice that a series of Solar Mass Ejections were to be expected, and that some electronic equipment might be effected. To be sure it was the largest and last on record and as the world turned a couple of revolutions, computers everywhere crashed, and the bright opalescent inhabitants of the world in their millions turned to dust. Painlessly, silently and without fuss or bother, regardless of race, age, sexual preference, height, education, weight, creed or faith, humanity in every corner of the globe slowly precipitated upon lawn, carpet and pavement like a congregation of weary phantoms laying down to rest.

I had driven to Ilfracombe for books, Scotch and other vital supplies, and parked up wishing my life would take a turn for the better. Wishing Becky was alive. Wishing I were dead. One moment the prosperous tidy streets were thronged with busy happy people who bounced along with that snappy, bouncy gait that marked out people with new blood. I shall never forget the look of pity in their eyes as we passed on the street. To them I would have looked dull, slow and ill-kempt; a dosser down on his luck, with dirty beard and worn boots. Within half a minute I was the briskest person in town; a town which had fallen silent. All about me people had turned to dust inside their clothes and as a slight breeze off the ocean sprang up, it blew their remains around in little eddies at street corners like miniature tornadoes. It began to rain and within the hour there was nothing human that was not represented by piles of wet rags, odd shoes and rivers of mud in the gutters. Stunned I loaded my beaten-up Land Rover with free groceries and cases of Scotch and drove home to get drunk once again.

It was a full week of hangovers, lashing rain and high spring winds before I ventured out again to see what sort of world I had inherited, knowing that I should have to share it with Jehovah Witnesses, ultra-conservative Jews and Muslim Extremists, not to mention bitter, old, anti social, short-tempered recluses such as myself.

What the future held for mankind there was no imagining. On more than one occasion sitting in my new Range Rover, or standing at the picture-window of my newly acquired luxury bungalow looking out through rummy eyes at a blood red sun sinking beneath the far horizon I would sometimes mutter. Sometimes shout. Bloody Hell!

God help all of us now.

# THINGS THAT GO BUMP IN THE NIGHT

On the far side of town a train rattled over wet points taking the last of the day's workers home in the hugga-mugga smoky atmosphere of its second class carriages. Its dim orange lights were just bright enough to read damp newspapers by, and its windows grey with condensation.

On the dark river tug boats hooted through the foggy air like melancholic territorial owls, and rain pattered against the back bedroom window of 43 Trafalgar Terrace, tucked away behind the streets, which were behind the streets, which ran between Camberwell and Peckham.

Straining his eyes in the darkness, Billy Deacon stared at the curtained window, lighter perhaps by half a degree than the room itself. A small room it was. A room dominated by a towering wardrobe built perhaps by giants for trolls and goblins to hide in, or so he believed. A board creaked, as boards in old houses do when settling down for the night. If that were not enough to chill the soul, there was something evil, something shapeless and dark between the curtains and the window. The harder he stared, the more he became convinced that it was moving. Slowly, so very slowly, it moved; agonisingly slowly with diabolic cunning so as not to be noticed. If he even so much as blinked it would appear as if it had never moved at all.

He bit his lip, fear mounting with every heartbeat. His heart was racing like a train now. He could hear it through his pillow. Drummers in the dark heart of Africa never sent such messages loaded with doom and foreboding. He tried not to give in to his fear and bit his lip harder until tears registered their presence. Soon his bladder would betray him for the coward he knew himself to be. He held on, but only just. A long drawn out second later his nerve broke, and he began to cry, and cry and cry and cry.

"There he goes again. Go and see to him."

"It's your turn. All he wants is a cuddle from his mummy."

"Well his mummy has to take his little sister to the clinic in the morning, you go. It's only another nightmare."

"Look Alice. Oh bloody hell, all right. Your feet are like ice, I'll go. No need to push. Oh bloody slippers."

"All right. All right, Daddy's here."

With the arrival of his father, the bringer of electric light, his heart returned to its normal routine rhythm.

"Another nightmare I suppose. What is it this time? Spacemen or ghosts?"

"There, Daddy. There behind the curtains."

And behind the curtains when pulled back? Nothing.

"There is nothing there Billy. There is nothing there in the dark that wasn't there when the light was on. See?"

Then to prove the point he switched the light on and off and on and off a few times but he could tell from his son's expression that logic was not going to be the route of the child's enlightenment.

"Look Billy, Mummy and I can't always be getting up every time you have a bad dream. You're a big boy now, how old? Nearly six. So this calls for drastic action. You know what I am going to do? I am going to ask two of my very best friends to stay here in your room with you. How about that? To be here with you whilst you sleep and see that you come to no harm."

Billy wasn't at all sure that he liked the idea of sharing a room. After all, having had the baby's cot here for just a few nights had not worked out at all well. He shook his head, but before he could articulate his protest his father continued.

"Oh you'll like them. They are two famous warriors. I have known them for, oh donkeys' years and because you are my little boy, and they owe me a favour, you can call on them at any time to come to your aid, at any time night or day. Their names are Courage and Imagination. Now Courage is a big strong chap, much bigger than me and wears a suit of blue steel armour. Arrows, knives, even bullets just bounce off. Nothing can touch him. He has this great big shield called Patience and a huge broadsword called Justice. Not even the most evil-evil bad men can beat him in a fight. Just can't be done. Stronger than Superman he is and smarter than, ummmm er Robin Hood."

"Don't believe you. Don't exist."

"He does too. Just close your eyes and you can see him standing guard over all of us. You, me, Mummy and baby Chrissie."

He could tell by the tightly closed eyes and the grim smile that a film was running inside Billy's little head. The blue eyes opened suddenly. "Tell me about Imagination. Tell me about him."

"Well for a start it's not a him its a her."

"A girl!"

"Yes a girl."

"Girls can't fight."

"This one is different. She doesn't have to fight - she has special powers."

"Please Daddy tell me about her too. Is she pretty?"

"Oh yes, very pretty."

"Is she as pretty as mummy?"

"Oh yes, much more pretty than mummy. Smarter too. She wears a long, thin silk dress which is sometimes grey and sometimes red when she gets cross, and sometimes black and then she can banish, with a snap of her fingers or a wave of the little white hand, even the most horrible evil spirits or bogey men. You know the sort of thing; the ones, like the thing you thought was hiding behind the curtains tonight. They all are just a bit silly, but they can't hurt you, not ever. Just keep you awake sometimes. If they do all you have to do is call up Imagination, and she will send them packing double quick, you see if they don't hop it smartish. No matter how strong they think they are, and no matter how strong you think they are, Imagination is even stronger so you need never be frightened ever again. With Courage and Imagination here beside you in you room, Mummy and me in the next room. With Uncle Colin and the whole of the Metropolitan Police Force clomping up and down outside with their truncheons and great big hobnailed boots. With an enormous army, navy and air force guarding us with guns and tanks and stuff, what on earth could you possibly have to worry about that might make a big boy like you cry?

"Now off you go to sleep. Oh you are asleep. Shagged out by all that howling I expect. Goodnight dear boy. I love you, you little bugger, and I have to face Mr Cattamole of human resources at 9:00 tomorrow. All nonsense really, just because of a bit of a prank in the stationary cupboard."

As he stood up to return to his own bed he saw his wife framed in the doorway.

"Oh Jimmy," she said. "What wonderful things to say to the child. You old softie – come here."

With that, she gave him a long tender kiss on the lips. Then suddenly her mood changed abruptly, as it will with women from time to time, and she stepped back.

A cat with its tail caught in a slamming washing machine door would no doubt have displayed similar emotions upon its features at the sudden change in its personal circumstances.

"What was it you were getting up to in the stationary cupboard and with whom?"

"And who exactly did you have in mind that wears thin, silk dresses and has such slender lily-white hands, and is so very much prettier and so much smarter than dull, ugly, stupid old mummy? Answer me that then you, you -----."

He could tell she was cross.

Swiftly, with the speed of a bounding lion Courage leapt to his rescue with his great sword and shield, deftly turning aside the deadly lance point of suspicion.

"No-one dear," he replied.

"It's just Imagination."

# SYLVESTER

S t Mary's campus looks particularly attractive at this time of year with the horse chestnut trees turning to gold, and the low autumn sun transmuting the dusty old red brickwork to an intense vermilion; a tint it is most reluctant to display at any other time of year. The new semester would be starting soon, indeed had started already in some departments, and fresh-faced young girls in sandals rode their bicycles to tea at Ma Green's on the high street where a little later impecunious students would wait upon tables, or play well-practised pieces of Bach and Mozart amongst architectural potted palms.

The cleaners and painters had been in during the summer recess and my office smelt fresh and new. I had a new desk, well not new; the retiring Dr Prentice had bequeathed it to me. Even so it took a bottle of fine old brandy before Phillips the head porter could be persuaded to move it into my office, and lose – somewhere - my old metal one. Small as such symbols were, they were the very currency of status in the groves of academia. Not that it was small. It was huge, made of fine red maple; an unusual choice of wood in such a piece of furniture. Seated grandly behind it, I thought of all I had achieved and would achieve in the years to come knowing full well that such speculations are invariably a foolish conceit.

Positioned in the centre of the worn leather scriven sat a green case file with a note from Fanshaw attached with a treasury tag. It read:

> Dear Jacob,
>
> I trust that you are fully refreshed after your long holiday in Europe, for I would like for you to take over one of the most interesting cases you could wish to find. I am very much afraid that I shall miss Founders Day gaudy this year as I go under the knife on the 28th. They say, as they always do, that it is just a routine procedure, but at my venerable age one never knows. Good luck to both of us then. I shall expect a fulsome report in your inimitable style upon my return to full health and duty.
>
> Yours
> Earnest Fanshaw

I ran a new, bright yellow duster around my desk, pointlessly for the desk, like the room, was spotless. I put on a pot of coffee to perk on the single antiquated gas ring in the cupboard kitchen, and as the aroma of fresh Blue Mountain coffee filled the room sat down to glance, no more at that stage, through Fanshaw's scrawled notes.

Maria, the subject, was twenty-five years old with an IQ of 180 and was working for her doctorate, which she was sure to get. Single minded, attractive and by her own admission a heterosexual virgin, spiritual but not a church goer. All things considered she was regarded as a well-balanced young woman who ran, swam, fenced and rode for her college. Very self-aware, she approached Fanshaw three months ago with a singular problem, which she recognised as having rather serious psychic implications.

For one day a month she became a man.

Once a month she would wake up and immediately begin to think, and to a certain extent behave like a man. On the first occasion she viewed her own naked body in the large wardrobe mirror, it was with a voyeuristic fascination. She looked at other women through new, yet familiar eyes. She drove her little car more aggressively and generally dared the world to come on and do its worst. She would frequent women-only clubs like the Silver Sisters on Bush Street, feeling that as a man she had no right to be there. She formed quick and easy relationships with the women customers, and ended up sleeping with them, sometimes two or three at a time. It was, she would tell herself, all a fraud and a bit of a lark. But the following morning, as her own person, when the spree was over she would remember every detail with a shiver. She began to set her thoughts and recollections down in a little notebook, which she called her journal of the Mr Me. Surprisingly she felt no self-loathing, merely amazement at such behaviour. It was, she said, analogous to a person accustomed to the occasional glass of dry sherry finding themselves, upon awaking, to be in a phone box on a country road stinking of urine and surrounded by empty cans of strong cider.

Tests revealed that her libido was, if anything, a little lower than normal, but not below what you might expect from analysis of her situation which was framed by single-minded study, and a concomitant solitary existence. Of homo-erotic impulses there was no evidence whatsoever. But for her monthly condition, one could conjecture that there was nothing in her mental make-up to give a doctor any cause for concern. Were it not for her voracious appetite for work and her high IQ she might have been any woman, anywhere, at any time. In his case notes Fanshaw mentioned something he thought noteworthy, which she occasionally referred to as Sylvester. She knew nobody of that name, but when pushed said that sometimes the name would float into her conscious mind initiating a panic attack which would last several minutes.

He concluded his notes by once again mentioning his forthcoming hospitalisation and suggesting that hypnotherapy might be the key to unlocking this patient's mind and restoring her equilibrium.

Hypnotherapy isn't a variety act but a medical skill requiring dedication and training like everything else in the field of medicine, and as you would expect a great deal of responsibility is placed upon the practitioner. It goes without saying that it can be a very dangerous tool in the wrong hands.

We met for a coffee and a Danish the following day, and spoke of Shakespeare, Jung, the Bible, the Upanishads and Three Day Eventing. We started therapy the following week. She readily agreed to drug-induced hypnosis and I gently led her back to her first memories and year by year, session by session we journeyed together towards the present. Whatever the cause of her problem, it was not rooted in her childhood or her adolescence. At length we arrived at the present year. January, February, March. Something was wrong. Her body stiffened and her breathing became laboured and shallow. Suddenly she began a one way conversation with Sylvester. Her responses comprised mostly of no's, a yes or two and ended with "Not again. Please leave me alone, please god. Oh help me. No, not, not, never."

I would have liked to have gone further but I dare not as she had begun to convulse. I neutralised the Pentothal with a shot of vitamin C and muscle relaxant, let her rest and put on a fresh pot of coffee before bringing her round."

"6, 5, 4, easier and easier, smell the coffee. 3, 2, 1, and you hear my voice, such a peaceful sleep. When I snap my fingers you will be fully awake and refreshed and all will be well. Then we shall have some coffee together."

Hallowe'en had come and gone before I felt ready to bring Maria into my office again. First I had to build up her will to resist and trust only my voice. I was her doctor and her friend. I would be with her in any future encounter with Sylvester. Together we were invincible, stronger than he could possibly be.

One thing I hoped to try was to put her under on a day that she thought that she was a man. When it eventually happened I was ready. There was a new tape in the recorder, Dr Anderson and Dr Arnold on call just down the corridor, and a nurse in the outer room.

Her voice changed completely when under, it was without doubt a masculine voice. Snappy and rather angry.

"Who are you?" I asked.

She groaned as if settling into a body that was far too small.

"Sylvester of course and you must be the meddling doctor - her friend. Yes. Well I suggest that you mind your own business because you have no idea of who or what you are playing with here."

"Perhaps you will explain," I asked as calmly as I could.

"You might as well try to explain DNA to a Hottentot. Talking to a low creature like you would be equally pointless for me. You think that you are so clever with your guns and chemistry and radio, but you know nothing. So back off Doc before, before …" He paused. "Before it becomes necessary to put you in your place. You call yourself a scientist but you know nothing. A blind worm trying to understand the stars."

"I can't do it you must realise that. She is my patient and in my care."

I hoped that at some level she was hearing this exchange and was aware of my commitment to stand by her.

"OK Doc, on your head be it. Between us it could kill her you know. You fool, it could kill you too. You have no concept of the power levels involved in this sort of exercise. It is science beyond your wildest imaginings."

"And to what purpose are you putting this poor girl through this?"

"Purpose, you ask me my purpose. Do you think I could tell you? Would you give a loaded pistol to a child or an atomic bomb to an African dictator? For all your talk of equality, you know it is a construct and a sham. You are no respecter of honesty and no keeper of secrets for me. In a thousand years perhaps, but for now just get out of my way. Do not interfere further with my experiment or it will be the worse for you and sadly for your patient."

At this stage, based upon my training, I believed this possession to be no more than a projection of my patient's subconscious. When I had discovered the deeply hidden, long repressed cause I could begin to address the root of the problem and vanquish it like a bad dream. Well I was all too much in error about that. In fact my training helped me hardly at all. I became so involved with this case that I cleared my backlog of cases and re-read all my reference works on 20th Century archetypes. I read up on the published literature, caught the train to Oxford to hear the illustrious Dr Snelling give a talk on the history of possession and exorcism.

I was seeing Maria every day now for sessions which lasted nearly the whole day. How that poor girl ever found time to work on her doctorate I will never know. Slowly I began to build up, through hypnosis, her strength and her ability to keep her psyche intact and undamaged. She needed an anchor, and for the moment it fell to me to be that anchor.

She had not been Mr Me for over a month and did not sense the presence of Sylvester either, when asleep or awake. Things were looking up.

Until one afternoon at the end of a session, as I was about to bring her back, he spoke to me directly.

"Well, well, well Doctor, allow me to congratulate you. You have almost succeeded in taking her from me. I could over-ride her will and yours so very easily."

Maria gave, a little gasp and began to fight for breath as her face turned blue. After what seemed to be an age, he said, "I could, but I won't."

Maria's breathing returned to normal, her small breasts rising and falling beneath her old fashioned pink cardigan.

"It's dangerous, it's no fun and it would waste my resources."

"What resources might they be?" I asked, not expecting a reply.

"Very good Doctor. Ever the inquisitive scientist, but no. No I enjoy my little visits. My my, what fun may be had in a woman's body, but that is just a diversion. I have, as you might say, bigger fish to fry. I could have any human being I chose. I need someone highly intelligent, resourceful, strong and well-versed in the ways of your world. In many ways she was perfect. Still if I can't have her, I shall have you. How would you like that?"

"Over my ..." I blurted out.

"Over your dead body, you were about to say. Hardly. Now that would be silly. But, over your dead mind hum?

"You can do nothing to me." I replied. I almost wanted to laugh in his face until I remembered that I was talking to a patient; a most complex and imaginative one to be sure, but a patient nevertheless. This entire exercise was a production of her mind. Nothing more. I could not allow my professional integrity to be sidetracked by indulging in thoughts of demonic possession, or anything which even smacked of an outside influence.

"Can I not? I can but to what purpose at this time? Believe me doctor; I would rather have you as a confederate than an enemy. Let me see, how can I convince you? Some small miracle perhaps? No. You are a scientist after all, and I must play by the rules. Tell me what is the time please."

I turned to look at the clock above the fireplace.

"4:00," I replied.

"Are you sure?" he said.

"Yes," I said looking at my wristwatch in confirmation. Within a minute or so they agreed, 4:00."

"Are you very sure?"

I looked again and again. Both clock and wristwatch agreed it was three forty-five.
"Erm," I said.

"Yes, is that all you can say about my little demonstration? I would have thought a round of applause would not have been out of place. Making mental changes is one thing, playing with time is something else. I am fatigued. Bye Bye."

Maria awoke and asked the time also. It was five past five. We had our coffee as usual though I was in no mood for small talk as I sat behind my desk writing up my notes.

"Why Doctor!" she said, "I never noticed before that you were left-handed."

"Don't be silly of course I'm not left ---"

But I was. My handwriting had changed slightly, but it was still recognisably mine and I was writing effortlessly with my left hand.

Over the course of the next few weeks my life became a living hell. Clocks would slip back and forth, as would my reading of the calendar. I would put something down, a book or a cup, blink and find it in another place. I became right- and left-handed on alternate days. Sugar my tea two or three times or not at all, thinking that I had. I could call for a brandy in a pub and find that I was drinking Scotch.

Sylvester, wherever he came from had found that he could alter states of perception. I speculated, and I don't want you to repeat this. You know how touchy some folk can be when matters of faith are mentioned, but it appears to me that this was a process not too different to the miracles in the bible which all hinged, when you think about it on changed perceptions. Water into wine. Feeding the five thousand, raising the dead. Was the manifestation of Sylvester in this poor girl's mind, and I suppose mine also, no more than a challenge to look at our conceptions of reality in a new way. If say, enough sane honest people all agree that they saw or heard the same thing, it would be asking for trouble to contradict them. Did the hands of my wristwatch and the clock in my office actually move or did I think that they did?

At first I tried to counter the bouts of confusion I experienced by writing things down; lists and schedules, but even then I read things I had not written, or thought that I had not written, whilst other things appeared. Things were becoming intolerable. I thought that I was going mad. I got the strangest looks as I walked through the quod as if I had forgotten my trousers. At least I did not start to believe that I was a woman thank god, and hang around public toilets to pick up men of, that sort. Then again why need he have stopped there if he really wanted to mess with my mind? He could, I suppose, have had me thinking and behaving like a dog. My insanity was not clearly a part of his programme.

The extent of my sure and certain knowledge at this time was this:

1) Sylvester was a highly evolved being with some all too human characteristics.
2) His power and knowledge were considerable but not limitless.
3) His business with Maria was in some way part of an enquiry, which probably had a scientific motive.

)  His gender was male and he was not above mixing work with pleasure.
)  By our lights he was amoral.
)  He was ruthless and determined. He could have destroyed me but chose not to. Why? Possibly because there are things he may yet learn from us. Or because he is under some constraint imposed by others of his kind not to cause more suffering than necessary for his study.
)  I am reluctant to say that the mechanism of his control was mystic or telepathic but rather based upon some principle we know not of.
)  Creatures like Sylvester are either produced by, or operate through, the deepest and most profound layers of the human subconscious and it is there that I plan to meet him. Understand him if I can and destroy him if I cannot.

This very night I plan to inject myself with a strong cocktail of drugs. (You will find the prescription attached) which will leave my mind fully in control whilst my body reposes in a deep sleep. It will be the experience of a lifetime and the most consequential scientific expedition of all time. I expect to be away some days but if things should go wrong my will is with my solicitor, and there are various letters on my desk. Farewell. Wish me luck.

Jacob

All the above was written five years ago and for all that time my colleague and friend has been sleeping for a peaceful eight hours a night in the College Infirmary where brain scans show that he is very much alive. His body, which is to all intents and purposes, completely paralysed, is ageing of course and his beard, hair and fingernails continue to grow. During daylight hours his eyes are open and they appear to be following events not available to us. If only you could tell us where you are, and of the things which you have learned, mankind might be on the verge of a new enlightenment.

From time to time Maria will pay him a visit. Now a Doctor and a mother she will tell him of her day, of the children or read to him passages from *The New Scientist*, *Economist* or *Spectator*. She never mentions Sylvester and would never be seen anywhere near the clubs in Bush Street. Her "Mr Me" journal she has entrusted to me for safe keeping until Jacob awakes, when no doubt he will wish to continue with his enquiries into the phenomenon known to us as Sylvester.

# THE END

There may be a few places which are more desolate and lonely than a North Cornwall highway in the rapidly fading light of a winter's afternoon, with a loitering chill mist and a sliver of a moon glimpsed behind the bare and arthritic branches of moribund trees bent by a lifetime of servitude to the heavy-handed north west wind, but I doubt it. It makes me shudder even now though I have had half a lifetime to get used to it.

I saw the hazard warning lights from way back. On a long, empty, undulating road it would have been impossible to miss them with the car perched on the top of a rise. Cautiously I slowed right down. I had no wish to run over any of the bits which may have fallen off the stricken vehicle.

"There will now be a short intermission," I said to myself as I turned off the Bach Sonata being broadcast from The Royal Festival Hall on London's South Bank. I changed down into second and rolled to a halt in the middle of the road. "Hello, hello, hello what do I see here? A fair damsel in distress?" I muttered with the familiar piece of Bach still playing in my head. Well almost. She was not as pretty as she had appeared from a distance in the late afternoon gloom, nor as young as when viewed through the lens of an over-indulged imagination, but no dragon by any means; neatly dressed in a navy blue two-piece suit, patent leather court shoes and a Liberty's scarf.

Knightsbridge and Bond Street fairly oozed through every square inch of her exclusive hand-stitched tailoring and drew me like a rusty tin-tack to a magnet. But it was the fragile little girl lost look upon that gamin face which held my interest in much the same way that a mouse is transfixed by the glance of the cobra, or how a bright steel gaff will hold a salmon and lift it high into the air beside an ice cold Scottish stream, gasping and wondering what on earth was going on. But having said that I have always had a soft spot for large black saloon cars, the classic Rover P5 in particular.

"Hi," I said, winding down the window and leaning over against the pull of the seat belt. "Are you having a spot of bother?"

Silly thing to say really; the offside rear tyre shredded to bits and the wheel down on the rim. How long, I wondered, had she driven it like that? Miles no doubt. Perhaps she imagined that the deterioration in the steering would get better all by itself.

"Yes," she said. "That thing," pointing at the delinquent wheel, with a mobile phone the size of a house brick in her hand, which they all were back then you know. "And this thing too."

Ah ha! The phone was in on the conspiracy too was it, but I didn't feel it wise to say so.

"I tried to call the RAC but it won't work here."

"No network coverage," I said very knowledgeably. "Here try mine."

She reached out a delicate hand. Things were looking up. At least it was not a boyfriend or husband she was trying to contact in her hour of need. No wedding ring either. Like most men I have a sort of radar which registers these details without even thinking.

She held up my phone like it was hot, filthy or radio active.

"Oh." she said looking up. I noticed that her eyes were hazel.

"Er...."

"Yes?" I replied.

"Er, Mr, er-m."

"Jim"

"Well Mr. Jim. You're not a terrorist or something are you?"

I thought, was this woman all there? "Of course not, don't be silly."

But hold on James old son. That accent; very English of course, but did I detect something in the way she said "terrorist"? Not Belfast exactly. Educated, private school, County Armagh perhaps. What if she were some sort of terrorist herself and planned to use my phone to ... No the idea was preposterous. Still if the police, MI5, SAS, Special Branch were picking up signals they would pretty soon trace it back to my phone and .....

Suddenly my handset went dead too, and she returned it with a sigh.

It was really dark now and getting colder by the minute.

"Well, look, never mind," I said. "If you hold my torch it won't take me a jiffy to change that tyre for you. If you have a spare that is."

"Oh how kind," she said with the sort of fawning feminine gratitude which I had always found utterly charming, not to say disarming.

"Erm, Mr. Jim. I'm awfully sorry, but I really must ask. Have you ever been in trouble with the police? Look at me now. I shall know if you try to lie to me."

"Eh-er No, no never but why should you think ...." I let it trail off there. I was beginning to think that this one wasn't the full shilling as we used to say back then.

Boy, don't I attract 'em, one after another, rich or poor? Looney women seem to single me out for special attention. Long ago I concluded that it must be pheromones, animal magnetism or something. One day I told myself. One day I will meet an attractive woman who isn't already half way round the bleeding bend, and I won't know what to do or say. No experience of sane women; won't be able to handle it. Go off my chump, wordless and gawping like a fish.

"Oh, never mind," she said. I sensed embarrassment. "Silly of me to mention it. I'm sure it will be alright."

I took the keys and opened the boot and began to unload the old, but top quality leather suitcases. Struth, the last one weighed a ton. I heard a metallic clink and convinced myself that I had been right all along. She was a terrorist. Her cases were full of Semtex and AK 47 Kalashnikov machine guns. So with my handkerchief I wiped my fingerprints off the handles as discretely as I could.

"What are you doing?" she asked accusingly.

"I thought I felt something sticky on one of the handles, that's it, all gone now."

"As long as you weren't wiping off your fingerprints."

Sometimes a red-faced second can last an eternity. An owl broke the silence and reminded us both that it was getting late. Motor maintenance was obviously not a matter of priority in the life of this lady, for the spare was almost bald although it held a pressure. I set up the jack and began to wind.

"I hope that you are well insured." I said, meaning to lighten the atmosphere which was thickening with mutual suspicion every second. "If it slips I mean, and crushes my leg, or something."

"Oh," she said. "I hadn't thought of that." Settling into a thick suede jacket with a lamb's wool collar, which she retrieved from the back seat, she shivered into it delicately.

"I'm sure it will be alright, if you are a qualified motor mechanic that is. You are qualified aren't you?"

"Only as an accountant, but enough of a mechanic to change a wheel for you."

"Ah well, the thing is if an unqualified mechanic works on my car it might effect the insurance or warranty or something. Leastways I think it does, and for that matter I am not sure of my liability under health and safety legislation either but if you have been on a course …..?"

"Er, no, no course. No qualifications in automobile engineering whatsoever."

I was working as quickly as I could. I was getting cold, my hands were dirty and I was getting fed up with this conversation. Things were not going as I imagined that they might. So much for gallantry.

I am sure that she was thinking aloud when she said, "What about employers liability?"

"But I don't work for you," I said, perhaps a little sharply.

"But you are working for me now aren't you?"

"Well let's talk about wages then shall we before I go on strike?" I said, too cross to laugh at all this nonsense.

"Oh you wicked Machiavellian; you plan to get me through the EU directive on minimum wages and working conditions," she said.

My god was she for real?

"Well come to think of it Mrs."

Heaven knows where that came from. I never call people 'Mrs' like that; some atavistic, serf and mistress emotion bubbling up from deep in the racial memory. "But you're right, this is hardly a safe working environment. Not in anybody's book. You haven't even put out the mandatory red triangle 50 metres back."

"Oh," she said. She said 'Oh' quite a lot and she really had a very pretty little mouth. She fished the triangle out of the boot and set the car rocking in its jack. I was not quite finished.

"Steady on. If that jack slips and your car falls on my foot we shall have to spend the night here."

Quite clearly the notion of spending a night in the dark with a stranger brought uninvited thoughts into her head, and even in the dark I could feel, if not see, her blushes. It took her long seconds to realise that a potential rapist with about a ton of classic motor car on his foot was no threat to anyone. She could also have driven off in my car to leave me to die of exposure, which was a threat – to me that is.

ATCO & Grass and other short stories

tightened the wheel nuts one more time and lowered the car back down. "Well, that's that," I said. "All done," as I dropped the wheel with its afro haircut into the boot and heaved up the suitcases full of god alone knew what mischief. It could be hard work, this knight errant business.

Then with a suddenness which startled us both a police car appeared out of nowhere its siren screaming and whooping blee-ba, blee-bar, blee-bar; its blue and white lamps  pulsing to set the heart beating.

Both of our faces must have registered equal amounts of horror and relief, but they were not after this little latter day Mata Hari and her gullible dupe with a car full of guns this trip because they just kept on going at full pelt. Well it was tea time and this was North Devon, well Cornwall.

"Mind how you go," I said, wiping my hands on my handkerchief, now ruined. "Remember that you don't have a spare any more, and that one is well below the legal limit."

"Oh," she said yet again, and if I live to be a hundred I will never know how a 30- something woman can look so like a frightened child.

"Perhaps it would be safer if you drove it."

Safer for who, I thought. "And what, you drive mine?"

"Yes, much safer don't you think?"

I must be a right mug, as I heard myself saying, "Well alright then."

I made a mental note not to touch things and to wipe the steering wheel afterwards. Seriously though, what if there were guns, or – worse - drugs, in the back there, what would the police say? Would they believe that I drove the car with the owner's consent; believe that I had no idea what was in the suitcases? It all sounded a bit lame to me and I was not a policeman out for a quick result. She interrupted this disturbing chain of thought.

"You do have a full licence and insurance to cover you to drive my car?"

"Do you, to drive mine?" A sort of stalemate ensued, one of mutual suspicion. I do not know who moved first or fastest when - putative tea-break over - the police car raced back in the reciprocal direction.

What I had experienced in the last fifteen minutes wasn't rational but rather strange, and still I couldn't put my finger on it. Something like a carnivorous worm was chomping away at my fund of good sense. I had to admit to myself that there was a large part of me which would have agreed to help her field strip, and clean her armoury in the boot if she were to ask me to do it, and look at me the way she had. So I followed obediently wondering what I was letting myself in for. We drove along dark and twisting country lanes for what seemed like an age the old headlights of her Rover bathing the road ahead in pale orange light. I wondered what she would be making of my car with its snappy performance, power-assisted brakes, and hard white halogen headlights.

We turned into a bumpy side road and through a wide gateway onto a crunchy gravel drive Two huge dogs bounded up to the car with its unfamiliar driver, all teeth and enthusiasm spoiling for an unequal fight. With a barked command to the dogs to be still, she turned to me with a pre-emptive, "Leave the cases." She walked with small steps up to the dark nail studded front door as if she owned the place, which she did of course.

The hall was enormous by any standard, with a log fire crackling nicely in a grand Tudor fireplace which spilled its arc of light onto a glass-eyed polar bear rug.

She flipped an old-fashioned brass switch, and a dusty chandelier anointed the oak panelled walls with buttery light. The walls were festooned with muskets and swords, interspersed at intervals with paintings of dour old ancestors. Who? What, where was this place? On her home ground she seemed to grow in stature somehow, and managed to leave all her insecurities behind up on the main road. Her mask of aggression, which she used to hide a very real nervous diffidence, drained away.

As if we were old friends she slipped off her shoes and stepped into threadbare slippers, pulling pins from her hair and shaking it loose as she did so. She was not just attractive, she was beautiful.

She pulled a silk rope by the fireplace, the sort you only ever see in old movies. A maid, au pair or whatever, appeared out of nowhere, trailing an aroma of onions and coffee.

"Ah, Sofia. Tea and toast for two in the library if you please, and perhaps a slice or three of Dundee cake. Is my father home? No? Pity I should have liked him to meet my friend Jim who put up with a lot of my nonsense on the main road when he was only trying to help a damsel in distress."

"Damsel? Que? What is damsel?"

"Never mind, Sofia I will explain later. Now, the tea."

I knew then, if I did not know before, that this was a woman I would sell my soul to the devil for. My mouth dried up, and very ordinary words crystallized like salt. My stomach, when it had finished chasing butterflies, clenched into the size of a walnut. I had never known a pain like it. My hands trembled and my legs turned to jelly.

She would say afterwards that I passed out and had to be revived with smelling salts and brandy, but I do not recollect it. Beastly stuff, smelling salts. The rest is history of course, and that boys and girls, is how I met your grandmother.

Lightning Source UK Ltd.
Milton Keynes UK
UKOW05f2146210115

244866UK00001B/15/P